D0287914

Lights, Camera, Amalee

Lights, Camera, Amalee

Dar Williams

SCHOLASTIC PRESS • NEW YORK

 Published by Scholastic Press,
an imprint of Scholastic Inc.,
Publishers since 1920.

Library of Congress Cataloging-in-Publication Data
Williams, Dar.
Lights, camera, Amalee / Dar Williams.— 1st ed.
p. cm.
Summary: When seventh-grader Amalee uses an inheritance
to make a movie about endangered species, she discovers
a link with the mother she never knew.
ISBN 0-439-80352-7 (hardcover)
[1. Cinematography—Fiction. 2. Motion pictures—Production
and direction—Fiction. 3. Endangered species—Fiction.
4. Interpersonal relations—Fiction.
5. Mothers and daughters—Fiction.] I. Title.
PZ7.W6559245Li 2006
[Fic]—dc22 2005028743

12 11 10 9 8 7 6 5 4 3 2 1 6 7 8 9 10 11/0

Printed in the U.S.A. 37
First edition, July 2006

Typography by Steve Scott
Book was set in Clarion

For my most tiny and colorful
tree frog, Stephen

Many thanks to the people who helped with the science of everything: Shelia Sinclair, Melissa Loge, and Jime Rice at the New England Aquarium, the Audubon Wildlife Sanctuary in Wellfleet Bay, Chris and Didi Raxworthy, Sarah Gubbins (and Chicago Research Support), and the Museum of Natural History. Also, thanks to Patty Romanoff, Nerissa Nields, Melinda, Pete, and family, the Flanagans, Patty Larkin, Bette Warner, Ruby and Rosa Xiaodan, Ron Fierstein, Jennifer Coia, Sacks & Co., David Levithan and all the friendly help from Scholastic, and the Robinson and Williams families, especially Michael.

✿ CHAPTER ONE ✿

The Little Story that Led to the Big Drama

What is it about the end of the school year that makes school almost fun? Is it the way you can just roll out of bed and get dressed in ten seconds — T-shirt, shorts, sandals — instead of half an hour? Or is it the feeling that school is officially over once the world looks and feels like summer? How was it that after everything that had happened in seventh grade, the wars between popular girls, teachers erupting in anger, and quiet kids finding all sorts of crude stuff written in permanent marker on their lockers, we could end with a sort of truce?

From what I'd heard, I'd gotten a break, because I had the best teachers this year, the least fed up with us, except for our math teacher, who'd had two temper tantrums, and the sewing teacher, who'd had one blowout and never seemed to like us again. Mostly, our teachers seemed to know that we were twelve years old and were surprising even ourselves with our bad behavior. They tried to work around it.

I also felt lucky that I'd helped with the lights and props for our school's production of *Fiddler on the Roof*, in which my friends Sarah and Marin had acted. Sarah was in a couple of my classes, too, and she turned out to be the anti–seventh-grader, the eye of the seventh-grade storm. She didn't even seem to notice the way all the kids were behaving, didn't see all the badly drawn body parts on the bathroom walls, or the gangs of girls yelling insults at some shy boy and then running away, or the gangs of boys getting chased out of the pizza parlor by the owner.

And then, as the days got warmer and lazier, it wasn't just Sarah. We all seemed to calm down. My English teacher, Mr. Chapelle, did things like send us out with tape recorders to interview people. It was an assignment that we all liked more than we'd expected. Sarah was especially brave about it. She chose to interview a truly nasty woman who worked in our library, and the whole class laughed as we heard Sarah asking one polite question after another while the woman got angrier and angrier, finally saying she had to go smoke a cigarette. Even Mr. Chapelle smiled at this.

It was in the last few days of school that we did the most amazing project. We had to tell a story. Mr. Chapelle said that it couldn't be written down, and hopefully it would show "the power of a different kind of language," whether it was the language of pictures, music, or spoken words.

I wanted to create a ghost story with the "language" of creepiness, which meant creepy music and special lighting, as well as a suspenseful story that I would read out loud. I dug around and found a photograph I remembered of a boy seeing that his hands had become bundles of knotty roots. It was from a book of pictures by Arthur Tress, who tried to photograph dreams and nightmares that children had had. He'd asked this boy to put on a coat that was longer than his arms, then stuffed branches into the sleeve openings and told the kid to just remember his dream. The final photograph made me shiver.

I wrote my own story about a boy who was cursed by a witch-troll for stealing a treasure out of a magic tree. Then I got a couple of flashlights and a recording of some scary organ grinder music. I also tied together a big bundle of roots and hid a little lamp inside them that I would turn on when the boy woke up underground in the witch-troll's den. I wrote that the boy expected to wake up in his own bed, but (click on the lamp inside the bundle of roots) found himself alone in a shallow underground cave. I described how he felt even more terror as he heard the witch-troll approaching (turn on scary organ grinder music).

Mr. Chapelle let me get the whole thing ready in an empty classroom with no windows. I enjoyed stringing up the roots and setting the CD player so I could play it on cue. Mr. Chapelle said that if I liked putting together this story, I should get a movie camera. He said it was easier than ever to make a movie. Then he helped me set up the only other piece of technology we needed for my story: a little machine that would project the picture of the root-handed boy on the wall.

The class filed in with only a flashlight beam on the floor showing the way. It helped my nerves to hear everyone sounding a little freaked out already, having to find their seats in the almost-dark. I read the story slowly, which also helped to calm me, and I heard some very pleasing gasps when I turned on the lamp inside the roots. When, at the end of the story, the curse was complete, and the boy woke up in his own room with his hands replaced by the knotty roots, I turned on the picture of the boy, and I was thrilled to hear seven different shrieks from boys and girls — even Mr. Chapelle, I thought.

This guy named Curt followed my presentation. He did the coolest one, because it was so simple. He wrote a little fake opera about what had happened between his sister and his mom a few days before the prom.

For a "costume," he plopped a pile of brown yarn on his head and became his mother, singing, "I have an idea. I have an idea. You can stay out as late as you want, but I will driiiiiive. Yes, I will driiiiive you!"

Then he dropped yellow yarn on his head and became his sister, singing, "No, no, no, no, nooooo! This cannot be! This cannot be! Eric will drive. He is nineteeeeen!"

And then the brown yarn for his mother was back on and he was singing, "Nineteeeen? Nineteeeen? You never told me this! Are you out of your miiiiiiiiind?" Everyone was laughing.

Mr. Chapelle surprised us when he did the last story, a film he had made about his son's trip to Mexico to swim with dolphins. His son was autistic, and there is a theory that somehow working with dolphins helps autistic kids communicate. Mr. Chapelle challenged himself by letting other people narrate the film. His brother, who had done the research about the dolphins, talked to us from the airport. Another passenger heard him speaking about it and wished them luck. Mr. Chapelle even had his son hold the movie camera as they got on the plane. He dropped it, and I could see how nervous everyone was, just by hearing all the passengers rushing over to help. It was great. It was a language that was bigger than words. I couldn't believe Mr. Chapelle had chosen something so personal to show us, but it was probably the best lesson he'd ever given me. Everyone tried so hard to look bored in class, I couldn't believe he'd believed in us enough to show us his story.

We had been pretty awful at times, as a class. We didn't exactly deserve it. Mr. Chapelle ended the class by saying, "You have many stories ahead of you. Tell them with creativity, clarity, and integrity." I made a note to look up *integrity*. I also decided that if I ever got the chance, I, Amalee Everly, would follow his advice and make a movie.

✿ CHAPTER TWO ✿

The Woman Who Wanted to Talk with Me

When Sarah and I headed home to my house that afternoon, we walked in to see not only my dad but also two of his friends waiting for me, looking very serious. It was like Mr. Chapelle's assignment; their silence had a language of its own.

My dad had been extremely sick the year before. We thought, when it was all over, that it had been a simple virus that had turned into something else, but we never knew for sure. Had it come back?

Dad was looking out the window with a tired expression, as if he was trying to figure out how much the whole world weighed. His brown hair was always a bit wild, but now it made him look like he'd been pummeled in a windstorm.

His best friend Phyllis's long legs were stretched out,

with her feet on another chair. She had her head in her hands as if she had a terrible headache. His also-best friend Carolyn paced back and forth, not looking up, her thin freckly arms folded.

"Is everything all right?" I asked immediately.

Dad turned to me and said, "I just told Phyllis and Carolyn some weird news."

"A dying old lady would like to talk with you," Phyllis said, without looking up. "And your dad thinks it's a good idea."

I looked at my dad to explain. So did Carolyn.

"Somebody wants to meet you," he said. "Your grandmother. Sally's mother."

Sarah spoke up. "Your mother's mother?"

We called my mother Sally. She had died when I wasn't even a year old, after she had left my dad and me. Phyllis and Carolyn, along with my dad's other friends, Joyce and John, considered themselves to be like my moms. Whenever we talked about Sally, it was like we were talking about an old friend we'd fallen out of touch with. We liked her, but we didn't know her anymore.

We treated it like that because we didn't have any choice. That's what I thought, at least. There was no way to get to know Sally, so there was no use being sad about her. But Dad's news was different. I had a chance to see a piece of history that was in my blood. There was a living person who might look like Sally or talk like Sally. I had a grandmother.

"Why didn't you tell me Sally had a mother who was alive? Did you know?" I asked. Maybe Dad had only found out now.

Dad sighed. "I guess I knew."

He guessed he knew? As far as I knew, I never had any living grandparents. How could he keep this from me?

Dad didn't notice my frustration as he continued. "She wants to meet you, because she thinks she is dying."

"But she's a vampire, so don't hold your breath." Carolyn suddenly interrupted, arms still folded.

Phyllis peeked up and shook her head. "Carolyn, you aren't helping."

Did they *all* know about my grandmother?

Dad tried to explain Carolyn's disgust. "Your grandmother is a pretty tough old bird. That's what Carolyn is saying. The last time we spoke was right after Sally and I got married. We ran off and did it and then surprised your grandmother with the news. She didn't take it well. She hurled a bunch of insults at us about how we'd ruined our lives, told us not to expect a penny of support from her, and, I'm sorry to tell you all this, told her daughter not to bother showing up again. After you were born, we tried to get back in touch with her, but it was too late. That's the whole, awful story."

"No, the story continues now with a morbid twist," Carolyn said drily. "Because now she's contacted your father to say she wants to see you, Amalee."

"I'm telling you what happened so you can make an educated decision about whether or not to see her," Dad said.

"I wouldn't go," Phyllis said. "She doesn't deserve to see you."

"No, let her see how cool you are, and tell her how glad you are that she didn't interfere and mess you up like Sal — that she didn't interfere with you," Carolyn said.

"You think she messed up Sally?" I asked.

"She definitely played a part in Sally's problems," Dad said. "But you shouldn't go just to tell her that or to be mean to her. I don't think she has any idea how she acted. She would just say she was trying to teach us how to be responsible."

"*I'll* come along and tell her," Carolyn offered.

Sarah laughed. Dad said, "It doesn't have to be a big deal. She'd like to meet you. I don't want to cut her off the way she cut us off. That's why I'm even entertaining the idea of giving you the choice of whether or not to see her. She asked to see you. It's up to you."

Suddenly it didn't seem so clear. I had a chance to meet a grandmother, but she might have a tantrum like my sewing teacher and say awful things about me — or, even worse, about Sally or Dad.

Back in my room, Sarah closed the door and said, "You have to take a tape recorder."

"Hey! I don't even know if I should go at all!" I protested.

"You have to go! It's your grandmother," Sarah insisted, which helped me feel less crazy. You're supposed to want to meet your family, right? Sarah went on, "So what if she isn't nice? Treat her like an animal at the zoo. That's how I thought of the woman I interviewed for Mr. Chapelle's class. Your grandmother sounds so mean, I bet no one's ever dared to record her voice. It would be like capturing the call of the great auk."

Sarah confused me sometimes, and this was a perfect example. "What's that?" I asked.

"It's an extinct bird. It looked like a cross between a penguin and a vulture. Lost. The last one was seen over a century ago and we'll never know what it sounded like. But you have technology. You could take a tape recorder and capture the call of the poison-tongued grandmother. You're not afraid of her, are you? You have nothing to lose."

I went back into the room where Dad, Phyllis, and Carolyn had barely shifted position. "Let's get it over with before I lose my nerve," I said.

Dad paused, looking surprised. Then he got up from his chair and headed for the phone. "Let's get it over with before we *both* lose our nerve."

The next day, Dad, Phyllis, and I headed off to a small town in Connecticut, a couple of hours away from our home in upstate New York.

"She lived this close the whole time?" I asked, feeling angry again.

Dad sighed. "The actual distance didn't seem to matter. Are you mad I didn't tell you about her?"

I reminded myself that Dad was the kind of person who would protect me from hearing about a grandmother who I wasn't allowed to meet. Then I felt angry at my grandmother and had to remember Sarah's idea to turn her into a giant ugly bird teetering on extinction.

"Sounds like you had your reasons to keep it a secret," I murmured. I was afraid I'd be overwhelmed by all this new information and feel like a wreck when I got to my grandmother's house. I tried to focus on the small tape recorder in the front pocket of my blue Windbreaker instead.

The plan was that Dad and Phyllis would drop me off and wander around for an hour. Then we'd all go out for a late lunch. Dad said I could even get lobster if I wanted. I could tell he felt both nervous and miserable.

I watched the houses get bigger and farther apart as we drove into my grandmother's town. Just as we pulled onto a street where every house was very grand in some way or another, we started slowing down. We were there. Her house wasn't as big as a French castle or anything, but it was a pretty huge brick one. The long rows of windows had dark green shutters, and the bright white front door had white columns in front that went all the way up to the second floor. We drove into the white gravel driveway. This was it. I started stepping out of the car almost before it stopped. I kept on saying to myself, *The sooner I do it, the sooner I'm through it.*

Before I went to the front door, Dad got out and gave me a long hug. "I'm proud of you," he whispered before kissing my head.

"You said this wouldn't be a big deal, remember?" I insisted.

Dad bit his lip. "Absolutely," he said, playing along.

"She's a stranger. You'll meet a stranger and spend an hour talking with her."

"Sounds like one of Mr. Chapelle's assignments," I said, secretly clasping the tape recorder. Dad wouldn't be mad at me for taping our talk, I knew. I just didn't want to make him more nervous by telling him my plan.

I heard Dad's sneakers on the gravel behind me. "Why don't I come with you after all?" he asked.

"No, Dad," I answered. We'd already discussed this the night before. I didn't want him to surprise her and risk making things more uncomfortable than if I went alone. And also . . . I suddenly realized this was my grandmother and it was my business what I said to her. And with that, I was ready. I walked to the door and knocked the brass knocker. It was heavy, but I felt strong.

A nurse with a name tag that said HEATHER answered the door. Dad and Phyllis drove off.

"Hi," the nurse said brightly, "you must be Amalee. C'mon up. We just had a nap and some lunch. Can I get you anything?"

After hearing what a terror my grandmother had been, I almost felt sorry for her to hear this nurse talking about her as if she was a four-year-old. My dad had mentioned feeling the coldness inside the house, and he was right about that. The temperature itself was cool, the walls were all a very light, icy blue, and all the fabric on the polished wood chairs glimmered silvery blue or white. The sweeping, curved staircase was the color of frost. I searched the pictures and award plaques along the wall in the upstairs hallway for pictures of Sally, but I couldn't find a single one. Why not? Where were the clues about Sally? I felt a mammoth tug of curiosity, and I realized why Dad was so nervous. Being nice to this dying woman meant I couldn't ask questions about the daughter she'd cut off. Her daughter, my mother. I couldn't ask my grandmother about my mother. For a wild minute, I thought maybe my grandmother would want to talk about my mother, only to me. She would share stories, secrets, pictures. But no, there were no pictures of Sally on the walls. I'd just seen that. Sally wasn't welcome in this house.

"Here we are," Heather cooed quietly, opening a door. I held my breath, pushing my mind back to the idea that this was just a random stranger as I braced myself to see her . . . but we were only entering a room on the way into the bedroom. "I'll make sure she's ready," Heather said.

There was still no sign of Sally, but this small office was at least busier than the rooms downstairs. Maps, charts, and photos covered the walls. There was a long, yellowing photograph of a sailboat. There were three pictures of my grandmother and, obviously, my grandfather, one of them standing with President Reagan, one with the first President Bush, and one with President and Hillary Clinton. My grandmother didn't look like the picture I had of Sally. But then, with her hair pinned up on her head like a flat gray stone and dark red lipstick and powdered cheeks, she wouldn't look like Sally who had long, loose, unbrushed hair and no makeup.

I continued pacing around the room. There was a mantelpiece with small china figures on it, of dogs, teapots, tiny women with hoop skirts.

And, finally, in a corner there was a bottle that was almost as tall as I was, with an ancient label peeling off that said MOËT & CHANDON. It was a champagne bottle. And it was filled — *filled!* — with coins. I gulped and stepped closer, trying to figure out how long it had taken to get so many pennies, nickels, dimes, and quarters inside.

Heather burst into the room with a light laugh, as if my grandmother had cracked a good joke. "All righty!" she said, ushering me in.

The walls were, again, light blue. The bedspread was white, and my grandmother's body lay like a snow sculpture under the covers, propped up by crisp white pillows.

"Hello," she said slowly. She was the woman in the

photos, but her hair was as white as the pillows, and there was no lipstick.

"Hello. I'm Amalee," I answered.

"How do you do?" she asked.

"I'm fine."

"Would you like to sit down?"

"No, thank you." She opened her eyes wider, so I quickly said, "Okay, thank you." I sat in a chair Heather had put out for me.

Then there was silence. "I have a question," I said, forcing myself to at least unzip my Windbreaker. I put my hand on the tape recorder.

"What do you have there?" my grandmother asked.

I pulled out the tape recorder. "I was wondering if I could tape-record this conversation."

"Oh, my, how small it is," she answered. Then she pointed to it, and her finger looked like an old bird's talon. "You may," she finally said.

I didn't have any questions prepared ahead of time, and I could see that now she was expecting them!

I looked at my grandmother. She looked at me. She stared at me, actually. I asked when she and my grandfather had moved into this house. She said they had moved in 1969. I asked when she had started putting coins into the bottle.

"Pretty impressive, hm?" she asked.

"It's amazing," I told her.

"My husband and I returned from our honeymoon in Europe and found that bottle waiting with the doorman at our apartment in New York City. It was from my parents. They wrote that we should open it on New Year's Eve if we were still married. It was a joke, of course. They knew we were very happy. But we did throw quite a gala on New Year's Eve that year, and George and I made a real show of opening the bottle and pouring it, together, into what must have been a hundred glasses. More, I think." As she spoke, she seemed dizzy with the memory.

I didn't have to ask any more questions for a while. She told me that George had been doing well at the bank, and that he had been married once before, and she had not been married before. She'd been a secretary in one of the science departments at Columbia University, and they'd had friends who had told them they had to meet.

"And the rest was history," she said. They went for dinner at a steak restaurant close to his bank, and he had "impeccable" manners. He'd held the door for her and pulled back her chair. They both loved sailing and wanted to travel, and for their first anniversary, he'd surprised her with a boat that they then sailed up and down the Hudson River.

She said that when they'd moved into their house, she'd supervised the placement of the bottle of coins to make sure the moving men didn't break it. "George said that a bottle of coins looked frivolous and penny-pinching, but I saw it as a good-luck symbol. I had the girlish fantasy that if George ever lost his job, which of course he never did, we could pack our clothes, take our bottle of pennies, and sail away on our boat. Sally always loved that bottle." At the mention of Sally's name, my grandmother stopped talking.

After seeing how my grandmother had just cut off the conversation, I realized I was right about Sally. I was not welcome to ask more about her. Sarah would have asked, but I couldn't. My grandmother looked like she might not survive it. I watched her hands flutter in her lap as she stared at the wall.

I asked if the boat that they sailed up the Hudson River was the boat in the big photograph outside of her room.

"Oh, yes," she answered. "The picture's in poor condition, because it's clipped from a newspaper. I really should have had it photocopied. The newspaper photographer took that picture of us when we went to go see the wonderful old ships on the Hudson River at the bicentennial. That means the two-hundredth anniversary of this country."

“I know the bicentennial,” I told her.

“You do?” she asked.

“Um, yes . . . *bi* means ‘two,’ *cent* means ‘a hundred,’ so that means two hundred, and 1976 was two hundred years after 1776, which is when they signed the Declaration of Independence, even though George Washington wasn’t actually the first president until later.” I was scared that I was sounding like a know-it-all, but I wondered how she thought I could have my father for a father and not know about the bicentennial!

“That is correct,” she said quietly.

“It must have been a beautiful day, on the bicentennial.” I hoped she would continue, and she did, but as she spoke about the clean white sails, her friends who also had boats, and the fireworks and cannons being fired from the old, historic ships, I could hear her breaths getting weaker.

She stopped speaking. Then she turned her head and stared at me again. “Do you like history? Is that your favorite topic in school?”

I told her I liked history, English, and science, and I described as much as I could without feeling like I was just showing off. I was pleased that she smiled when I said I was looking forward to biology in ninth grade.

She looked like she was about to say something, but

instead, she took another long pause. The small plastic clock next to her bed showed that the hour was almost up, and I was scared about what would happen if we went on even longer. I decided to give her the opportunity to end the conversation, and so I asked what Mr. Chapelle called the summary question.

"I have one more question," I said. She raised an eyebrow. "Do you have a philosophy about life that you'd like to share?" I asked. It sounded very formal. "That's the question my English teacher asked us to ask when we did interviews with people this year." He'd said to ask for "*a* philosophy" so people wouldn't think we were demanding that they come up with their one and only philosophy, which usually scared them.

My grandmother had a glaring look about her, but simply asked, "So you enjoy going to school?"

"If you take out some of the other kids, yes," I answered too quickly. "I mean, my teachers are okay, and I liked what they were teaching, but the kids were . . . uh, confusing to . . . to me." What had I just said? I rushed on a bit and said that I thought I would enjoy school more next year and that I wanted to take French or Spanish, and that I wished I had taken it this year, but there was a problem with the schedule, but I heard that if you start when you're twelve or younger, you don't have an

American accent when you speak. On the word *speak,* I reminded myself to stop speaking.

"Biology, French, or Spanish . . . it sounds like you have some big plans for your life," my grandmother replied unexpectedly. Then she cleared her throat. "Would you like to hear a philosophy?" she asked, with a hint of amusement in her voice.

"Yes, I would."

My grandmother took another long, dry breath and said, looking at me, "Look at the world and listen to the world. We set out to teach everyone our lessons, but we need to be taught ourselves. I've watched closely in recent years. Without exception, I have learned important lessons from everything I have observed, from bees to humans. Unfortunately, I acquired the skill of watching and listening too late in life. I had already overlooked things and sacrificed them forever, losing whatever important wisdom they were sent to give me."

This seemed unusually nice and smart for the woman I had been hearing about. She started to close her eyes, and then fought to keep them open.

"I'll let you sleep," I said, standing. She lifted her hand slightly and let it drop.

"It was nice to meet you," I whispered politely.

"Hm," she responded with a slight nod of her chin.

I got up my courage, reached out, and touched her hand. In an instant, she grasped my hand in hers, clutched it, and let it go. She really *had* wanted to meet me.

Heather was waiting in the small office, reading a magazine. "Your father and his friend are waiting outside," she said. I looked out the window and saw them milling around the lawn, talking.

"She's asleep," I told Heather. "You may want to make sure she's okay."

"Oh, she's fine," she answered. "I hope she wasn't cranky! After I've shown you out, I'll make her some yummy cottage cheese and peaches."

I walked down the grand staircase and wondered about how a great auk would feel, after living such a fierce, free life, being told now that its behavior was "cranky" and being hand-fed "yummy" cottage cheese and peaches.

I wasn't sure I could believe she was my grandmother. She didn't look like anyone I knew, including me. We hadn't talked about Dad or Sally or anything like that. She seemed more like a principal who makes you want to be on your best behavior. Maybe I would have felt closer to her if I didn't know she could send me away at any minute if she disapproved of me. But I could tell she hadn't wanted to send me away. I could even say that she liked me.

✿ CHAPTER THREE ✿

Message in a Bottle

The confusing letter came a week later. "This is from your grandmother's lawyer," Dad began, skimming the stiff cream stationery. "Amalee, did you want to see your grandmother again?"

My first thought was *no way.* Was that rude? "To be honest, I was nervous when I met her. I don't have to do it again soon. Why? Does she want to see me again?"

"Actually, the reason I asked is that she seems to have been sicker than we thought."

"I could tell she was very sick, or at least very tired," I told him.

"Well, she was very sick, and now, Amalee, I'm sorry to tell you that she has passed away. She died a few days after you met her." He studied me to see if I had a reaction. "Are you sad about that?" he asked.

I didn't know what to say. I was secretly glad I had our tape recording. I also felt happy that I had shown her, once and for all, that Sally wasn't wrong to have married my father. Then I had a mental picture of my grandmother just before she died, thinking about her daughter and feeling sad, and then I felt sad, but I swallowed down the lump in my throat, because it all felt too complicated to describe my picture of an old woman looking out the window at the big tree in her yard and feeling sad. "I'm glad I met her," I said. "And I bet it was good for her to meet me, you know, like finally getting to read the ending of a book she'd started."

"Nicely put. And that's what you feel? Happy for her?" Dad asked suspiciously.

"It's not like she acted like a grandmother, Dad," I pointed out. "She didn't bake me cookies or take out lots of family pictures."

"Do you wish she had?"

I didn't want to admit how much I wanted to see some sign of Sally. "I don't know," I answered. "It's just that she didn't do anything to make me feel related to her."

"She was never particularly warm," Dad observed.

"She was not warm," I agreed.

Dad took one last look at me, then went back to the letter. "This isn't very warm, either," he said. "But it's from her lawyer, and lawyers are supposed to be businesslike and even annoying."

I smiled. "What does the annoying lawyer say?" I asked.

"Well, this letter is telling me right off the bat that I'm not getting any money, but that she instructed that you were to be sent a monetary token that is not a formal part of her estate." He sighed. "I'm guessing this means she wrote a check to you just before she died and made sure they sent it out before it could go through all the legal rigmarole that ties up inheritances."

A check? Before I could imagine how big that check could be, Dad warned, "Oh, boy. Maybe I shouldn't have even read this to you. She had a ton of money, but she made a point of saying that people should earn their own, so she rarely gave any away. She probably sent you fifty dollars, or maybe a hundred." That was a lot of money to me, I pointed out. "Or maybe twenty-five. Just don't get your hopes up."

"If I'm really lucky, she left me that house," I said.

"No, no, no!" Dad protested. "I don't think it's realistic for you to think that. The lawyer would have said —"

"I was kidding, Dad. I don't want her house. It's an icebox."

"Oh. You thought so, too?" he asked, smiling. He put the letter in a file of legal papers, and it only took up a small part of my imagination . . . until three days later, when my inheritance arrived.

Dad was at work, and I was deciding what to do with myself when the phone rang. I picked up the receiver and said hello.

"Uh, this is Ronny down at the post office. Is anyone home there?"

"I am," I answered.

"Yeah, well, is someone older than you there?"

Phyllis always said to never tell anyone that you're home alone.

"Of course there's an adult here. There are two," I exaggerated.

"Will they be home in the next hour? I have a very heavy package for an . . . Amy Lee Something?"

My heart beat faster.

"They'll be here," I said. How big could the package be? Was it some big book Phyllis had told my dad to order for me? She did things like that.

I went to the front window and camped out there until the mail truck arrived.

The postman jumped out, opened the back of the truck, and put something on a cart. I couldn't see it.

"Where are your parents?" the postman asked as I walked barefoot down the driveway to meet him.

I just said, "You can leave that out here on the lawn." I still couldn't see what it was.

He wheeled around a huge crate, bigger than a washing machine. I'd made a mistake — a big crate of a mistake. I'd never be able to move it myself. Still, I nodded to him when he brought it to a place in the middle of the lawn, letting him know he could leave the delivery there. Phyllis would kill me if I let him get too near the house, even in his uniform and even with the mail truck he was driving.

"You're going to have a hard time getting it inside," he muttered, straining to push the cart toward me.

"We have a cart like that. We can wheel it in," I told him.

And then he was gone, and I was alone with a big crate in the middle of a small lawn. This seemed like a good moment for a popular girl to pass by and say something mean, or . . . oh, no . . . Kyle, the totally great, nice, and gorgeous sixteen-year-old guy up the street. I looked out toward his house. No Kyle.

"Hi, Amalee."

I swung around and almost tripped over the crate. Kyle. "You're not home," I sputtered.

"What do you have there?" he asked. He had beautiful wrinkles around his dark brown eyes when he smiled.

"I don't know," I managed to say.

"You want to find out? Looks like it's addressed to you." He squinted to read the script on the label. "Do you have a hammer? I could pry this thing open."

"Sure," I said, carefully running to the garage. I brought back two hammers.

Kyle and I started tearing out the nails with the backs of our hammers. A minute later, the crate lid opened easily and I saw a glint of its contents. I didn't recognize it on its side, surrounded by dark confetti, but when I could see the basic shape, I knew exactly what it had to be.

This is what I'd inherited. I was looking at my grandmother's giant bottle of coins.

Floating around the top of it was a small envelope with the word *Amalee* written in big, friendly letters, the kind Heather the nurse would write. I opened the envelope quickly so that Kyle wouldn't have to stand there waiting. The note inside was written in shaky letters, my grandmother's letters. It said,

Dear Amalee,

I hope these help you pursue your interest in the world. I recommend you use them now.

Your Grandmother,

Suzanne Weston

"Wow! Who sent this to you?" Kyle asked.

"I inherited it from my grandmother. My dad told me she'd left me some money," I explained. Then I joked, "Just a little spare change."

"How does a person collect so many coins?"

"She's been doing it since after her honeymoon in 1966. Her husband was a big-deal banker. They believed in saving money."

"That's almost forty years," Kyle said. "What are you going to do with it now? Put it in the bank for another forty years?"

I reread the note. My grandmother obviously didn't want me to wait another forty years. "I'll see what my dad thinks. He can help me count them and stuff," I said, already feeling silly that this would be sitting in the center of my lawn for another two hours.

"Hey, I just got my license," said Kyle. "Would they count this for you if you took it to the bank?"

I was so horrified. The idea of sitting in a car with Kyle

and coming up with something to say was too much. I couldn't stand it. But I had to stand it. This might be my last chance to talk with him. I had to. I reminded myself that this was just Kyle, the nice kid who used to shovel our driveway on snowy mornings for a few dollars. I'd hardly noticed him until a couple of months ago when he'd brought our newspaper, looking like a sopping rag, up to the door one morning, bravely telling us that he'd run over it in the rain (the newspaper boy had clearly missed his mark). As he apologized for ruining our paper, I saw a cool, handsome guy with a sense of humor. He even admitted that he'd thought he'd run over a dog, so this was practice for coming to a doorstep with much worse news.

I'd told him that it wasn't his fault that the newspaper had been playing in the street without watching for cars. And then he laughed, and I saw the wrinkles around his eyes, and I was done for.

Suddenly I realized we were in the middle of a silence.

"Oh! Well, to answer your question, I know they count paper money for you at the bank," I said. "And I think I've seen them counting coins in those paper rolls, but you shouldn't do this." I'd come to my senses. This was way too much to ask.

"I'll get my truck and bring it down here," Kyle offered, already jogging away.

I watched Kyle disappear into his house and come out again, then slowly pull his pickup truck out of the garage and drive up to our curb.

We — mostly Kyle — used my dad's cart to heave the crate into the back of the truck. It was a small truck. We watched the whole thing sag.

Kyle bit his lip. "It's okay," he said quietly. We got in the front.

"So, you just finished sixth grade?" he asked pleasantly.

Stabbed with a rusty dagger! "*Seventh* grade," I said.

"Oh, yeah, right. How was it?" he asked. We were driving through town now, which suddenly seemed like an exciting place where teenagers drove around and hung out.

I told him how I really liked English and history and that I found out I liked science class, too.

"I would have liked science," Kyle told me, "but I was so bad at those experiments! We had to burn down a walnut and then do this equation about how many calories it had, and I came up with, like, a thousand calories."

"That was a hard one," I agreed. "I think I came up with a thousand, too, but so did the rest of the class."

"Really?" he asked. "That's amazing. I just remember thinking 'Okay, I'm just not good at science.' Maybe I gave up too early." He didn't sound upset. He sounded amused. "Girls who like science are cool," he added.

He couldn't have said anything nicer. I looked out the window and saw myself as a scientist with a lab coat and really cool glasses. I was explaining something to Kyle as he looked into a microscope.

Kyle found a space right in front of the bank. I told myself this was proof that going to the bank with him was the right thing to do. Kyle found an old sweatshirt in the back and we used it to drag the crate back onto the cart.

"Thanks, Kyle," I said, trying to sound close to sixteen.

"What are you going to do? Don't you need a ride home?" he asked.

"No, I'm fine. I can walk. And someone can come back for the bottle," I assured him, thinking that I could call Phyllis or Joyce or just walk down to John's restaurant for some help.

"I'll wait for you," Kyle said. "This is the first time I've driven since I passed my test. I mean, as soon as I got my license, I drove down to New Paltz and got a new wallet." He looked embarrassed that he had just admitted this. "I'll wait," he insisted, and stood at the back of the bank.

As I stood in front of the teller, I realized I hadn't come

up with a way to explain myself to her. "I got some money," I started. "I inherited it —"

"You have a check?" she interrupted me. I'd seen her before. She was always very businesslike, not especially mean, just All Work. Her name plaque said MONICA HAZLETT.

"No, I don't have a check."

"Do you have an account here? Did you want to open one?"

"No — I mean, yes. I have an account here, so I don't need to open one."

"What's your name?"

"Amalee Everly." *The scientist*, I thought. *Environmental scientist*. I hoped I was handling this well, with Kyle just standing there. "That's what I got," I explained, pointing to the coin bottle, which Kyle had stood up so we could see what was in the crate. I saw Leslie Scott's mother enter the bank as I turned. Leslie and I had been in a few of the same classes.

"Hi, Amalee," Mrs. Scott called. She looked at the bottle and then she nodded to Kyle, who nodded back. "What's up?"

"How did you get that in here?" Ms. Hazlett asked.

"I guess we dragged it in," I said. The sweatshirt, still

between the crate and the cart, looked like the crushed witch from *The Wizard of Oz*.

"Oh, no," Ms. Hazlett said with a sigh. "You'll have to take that home and count the coins yourselves. Here, I'll give you some coin sleeves." She leaned down to get them from behind the counter, then called, "What is it, mostly? Nickels? Pennies?"

Kyle spoke up, "It's okay. We'll just take it home to your house. I'll help you get it inside."

That's when I started to feel desperate, watching all this happen in front of Kyle and even Mrs. Scott.

"So," I stammered, "you don't have a machine or something that counts coins?"

"No. We don't." She pushed the pile of sleeves in my direction. Then she looked over my shoulder and asked Mrs. Scott, "Can I help you?"

So mean.

"Yes, I'm curious," Mrs. Scott said. "Haven't I seen those machines that count coins here? I'm sure I have."

"I'm sorry," Ms. Hazlett answered, "the bank doesn't count coins. We offered those machines as part of a promotion."

"But I saw them recently, didn't I? Don't you have some left over that we could borrow? Maybe I could count a pile for Amalee here. I've got a half hour before Leslie's soccer practice ends."

"We've got a few machines," Ms. Hazlett said, looking like she felt bad for being so impatient with me. "I guess I could count a pile, too. It's been a slow day."

"That's a good idea. I can do that, too," Kyle said. "If you've got an extra one for me to use, I mean." So polite.

Ms. Hazlett dropped the whole business look. "I don't think it will take long if we're all using the counters," she confided. "We could get at least part of the job done so you don't have to drag that whole thing back. What if the bottle broke? It's so beautiful, so old. I'll be right back." She went to a back room and brought back a cardboard box from which she plunked three coin counters on her desk. She took a pad of paper out of her drawer. "Shall we have a contest to see who gets closest to the actual contents of the bottle?" she asked, smiling. "I'm guessing one thousand three hundred twelve."

"One thousand three hundred twelve coins?" I asked, not believing what I was hearing.

"One thousand three hundred twelve *dollars*," she answered calmly.

Wow.

"This is really nice of you," I said, looking at everyone, though less at Kyle in case I blushed.

"It's no problem," Mrs. Scott said. "This is a little project. It should be fun!"

I thought Mrs. Scott should be friends with Phyllis.

Kyle hauled the bottle over to the desk, introduced himself, tipped the bottle on its side, and dumped out the first coins on the carpet. I started separating them.

"No need to do that," Ms. Hazlett said. "The machines will separate the coins, but since we only have three counters, you can be the one who puts the piles on the desk and clears the finished rolls away."

I put a pile next to her. "Here we go," she said, feeding coins into the top of the counter, which immediately started spewing them into different sleeves.

Mrs. Scott did the same, and Kyle started in on his own pile and said, "Cool." The sound of coins bouncing on hard plastic was soon echoing through the bank. I had plenty to do just dumping, piling, clearing out, and replacing. Within minutes I was making piles that looked like miniature truckloads of lumber.

We were already up to about thirty-five dollars . . . and we'd barely begun to empty the bottle. If this bottle of champagne once filled a hundred glasses, we'd only gone through about three!

Someone came in, and Ms. Hazlett jumped up to help him, but soon she joined us again.

"I love counting money," she confessed.

"Me, too!" said Mrs. Scott.

"I still feel like a kid when I'm adding up money from other countries," Ms. Hazlett added. "It's so colorful. I really like Australian money."

Kyle lifted up the end of the bottle and spilled a melting mountain of coins onto the carpet. There were a few dollars, folded around slips of paper. I unfolded the dollars and the slips of paper, which turned out to be old receipts.

They were all in computer printout mode, very clear. The first was Caldman's Pharmacy, June 20, 1999: prescription, prescription, cotton balls, knee brace. I started flashing on my grandmother in her house, pulling cotton balls from the medicine cabinet and keeping medications in the kitchen cabinet. What did she need them for? How long had she been sick?

Farther down was a dollar with a receipt from the same pharmacy from 1995: reading glasses, magazines, and tissues. Which magazines? I saw her sitting in the sunlit corner of the living room reading a ladies' magazine.

In fifth grade, an archeologist visited our school and showed us how archeologists carefully dig through layers of dirt, and how sometimes they'll find one whole history on top of another. There will be pots and broken plates from the early twentieth century in one layer and arrowheads in a layer farther down.

Here I was finding history buried in layers of money instead of dirt. There was a bookstore receipt, receipts from a couple of different supermarkets, and lots of pharmacy receipts.

"Hey!" Ms. Hazlett called out. "More dimes and quarter sleeves, and snap to it!'

"More quarters and nickels here," Mrs. Scott added. They laughed at my expression when I saw how many rolls had built up since I'd last looked.

"Sorry, I was reading these old receipts," I explained.

"Really?" Ms. Hazlett stopped for a moment. "That seems so . . . personal."

"It is," I agreed. "But it was my grandmother, so do you think it's okay?"

"It's absolutely fine," Mrs. Scott jumped in. "This is all yours. She left you a bottle, not a check. This is much more exciting, more romantic."

My face felt hot. She'd said "romantic" in front of Kyle. Luckily he was busy at his counter.

Mrs. Scott was still talking. "I think she wanted you to know about her. That's why she left you a thing instead of a dollar amount."

I thought again about the note. Mrs. Scott was absolutely right. The bottle made me think of my grandmother's life, about how she wanted to take the big bottle of coins and escape on her boat. Looking at the bottle made me think of her, and her dreams, and even about how she wanted me to have my own adventures. You couldn't do that just by writing a check.

"How much do you have so far?" Kyle asked.

I counted the piles, putting the rolls in groups of five. We had a little over four hundred dollars! Everyone got a little giddy over my report.

And we were down to 1981. The 1981 receipt was for the pharmacy again: magazines, toothpaste (three tubes), a toothbrush, and "sparkle hair clips." Sparkle hair clips? My grandmother was born in 1930. I did the math. She wanted sparkle hair clips when she was fifty-one? She didn't seem the type.

Who would she get them for if not herself? Suddenly my hand went weak. My mother. Sally would want them. Sally was eleven years old in 1981, almost my age now.

August 31, 1981, just before school was starting, right? Had my grandmother put up a fight? Were they red or blue? Maybe they were my grandmother's idea. Was my mother a tomboy?

I knew almost nothing about Sally. She was "a little wild," she had brown hair like mine, and she was not a mean person, according to Carolyn. John said she was "a friendly soul." I had secretly stored up everything anyone had ever said about her, but now I realized how little that was. She started college and meant to finish but never did. She had long hair. She was wearing a big sweater and a blue hat in the only picture I had of her. She left before I was a year old, but for some weird reason, no one was angry at her for it, maybe because she had died soon after.

Before everyone noticed I was out of commission again, I reloaded the coin sleeves and put a big pile of coins in front of each of them.

Ms. Hazlett had put the four hundred dollars aside so I wouldn't recount it. The new rolls were lining up again.

A long receipt from Grand Union, 1978, had a few standouts: a chocolate bar (for my mother?), cornflakes, bananas, peanut butter, and flowers. The receipt was from early April. Were the flowers daffodils? Were they my mother's idea? Did my grandmother buy them because she was in a good mood?

Farther down, in 1977, there was a receipt for a brush and shampoo from the pharmacy, but I saw something that I was almost too scared to read, handwriting on the back. It was a child's handwriting. Sally's handwriting. It had to be. She'd written a list of words: *Flower, Power, Shower*.

She'd crossed out *Mower*, having obviously realized that words with the same spelled endings don't all rhyme. She wrote *Sour* and *Tower*, followed by *Chowder and Powder in EMERJUNSEES*. I guess if a person was having a poem emergency, she could go to the words that didn't exactly rhyme. I imagined Sally camped out in the car, waiting for her mother, playing a game with herself. Did she want to write a poem? I could imagine a sweet seven-year-old kid. Was she?

"I have to go," Mrs. Scott groaned. "Rats! I wanted to finish the job!" I counted up the total so far. The second pile of money was two hundred ninety dollars, which I added to the other pile and got six hundred ninety-eight dollars and fifty cents. This was already more money than I'd ever had, and there was no end in sight.

"That's amazing," Mrs. Scott marveled. "What are you going to do with all this loot, Amalee?"

"I'm making a movie," I said.

"Really?" Kyle asked. He knew I had no idea before now what kind of money I was going to get.

I was very surprised, and then excited, that this was

my answer. I knew that when I saw Mr. Chapelle's movie, I had wished I had a movie camera. "Yeah, I'm making a movie," I repeated. It would be my first project as an environmental scientist. "Not a big one. Just a little one."

"I'll tell Leslie, if you like," Mrs. Scott said. "She's going on a canoe trip in July, but she loves making costumes and clothes on my old sewing machine. It's her latest thing."

"Excellent," I said. Leslie had been one of the first girls in our class to have a real boyfriend — one in the eighth grade. I decided not to mention that this was her latest thing, too.

Mrs. Scott left after Ms. Hazlett promised she'd tell her if she won the guessing contest.

I had guessed three hundred and ten dollars.

I replaced Mrs. Scott at her coin counter and thought about my film while I watched the coins fly into their various coin-sleeve homes.

An hour later, the bottle was empty and Ms. Hazlett was counting everything up and putting the money into my account for me.

She handed me a receipt, which I added to the pile of receipts from the bottle. So this was what the day had brought: I was going to make a film. It would be about endangered species, I decided. And I had two thousand eight hundred eighty-one dollars and thirty-two cents to make it.

Would somebody look at that receipt and wonder what it felt like to be a twelve-year-old with that much money? They couldn't know about how Mrs. Scott saved me from embarrassment or that Kyle had been sitting next to me after she left and that it felt like there was a wave of electricity between our arms. But they'd know something important had happened.

Maybe everything changed the day that Sally got those sparkle hair clips instead of plain ones. And maybe this piece of paper, dated June 8, would be the record of the day my whole life would change, too.

✿ CHAPTER FOUR ✿

How to Spend a Fortune

Kyle drove me home. The empty bottle was easy for him to lift now. I tried to give him twenty dollars as a thank you, but he said I should keep everything for the movie.

"You gave up your whole afternoon!" I protested.

"It was fun," he said. "I had my last exam today and I had nothing to do before we go partying tonight. What else was I going to do — celebrate with an ice-cream cone?"

I laughed with him at this ridiculous idea. That's exactly what I would have done. I stared out the window.

How could I tell Dad about what happened in a way that would surprise him the most? It wasn't Dad at the end of the driveway when Kyle dropped me off, though. It was Joyce, jogging out slowly in her soft pink shoes. She was a therapist for teenagers, and she often had a look that said, "I'm *listening*. I *care*." It used to drive me crazy, but I'd gotten used to her perfumed, flowery, friendly ways. I had to admit that her therapy language and even her tricks had helped me when my dad was sick.

"Amalee!" she cried. "Where have you been? I saw your bike was still here, and . . . *hello*." The last word was directed at Kyle.

"Hi," Kyle responded shyly.

"What's your name?" Joyce asked sweetly but not very nicely.

"This is Kyle," I broke in. "He lives down the street. He drove me to the bank."

Joyce wasn't smiling.

"I just got my license," Kyle reassured her. "I'm a legal driver."

"Ohhh." Joyce looked relieved. "That explains it."

Explains what? I was too embarrassed to ask.

I got out of the car. Joyce and I watched Kyle slowly back out of the driveway, craning his neck to make sure there were no cars coming.

"You're fine!" Joyce shouted helpfully.

"Thank you so much!" I shouted as he drove away.

Joyce said, "What a nice boy."

Kyle had pulled into his driveway and run back out to the curb to pick up the empty garbage cans.

Even though Joyce had always told me she wanted to know what I was feeling, I knew I couldn't tell her that I was head over heels for a sixteen-year-old. But I did ask her what she'd meant when she'd said, "That explains it."

"Oh," she said breezily, "when people first get their licenses, they want to drive everywhere. So that explained why he would be driving a twelve-year-old into town."

"Couldn't he just be nice?" I asked.

"Maybe, but probably not," she answered without considering it. So that's where she stood: Kyle liked driving, not me.

Suddenly I felt two hundred years younger than he was. The only kind of older guy who would be interested in me would have to have something wrong with him. Where had I gotten the idea that he could see me as some cool girl shooting her own film?

"Where's my dad?" I asked. Now I wasn't sure I would even mention the idea of making a movie. Twelve felt so young.

"He and Phyllis are over at the restaurant." The restaurant was John & Friends, John being the chef and the rest of us being the friends who had helped him open it. Phyllis, for example, did the accounting. She loved to make order out of chaos. (I think her favorite words are "I have a plan.") In exchange for free food, she kept track of money going in and out of the restaurant, using a small laptop computer John had bought her. I once asked if she thought she was getting a raw deal doing so much work for no pay except free dinner.

"It's not just any dinner. It's *John's* dinner," she pointed out.

Phyllis ate at John's restaurant almost every night and brought a doggie bag to work the next day. She was the principal's assistant at my middle school.

I always loved hanging out at the restaurant. I felt like an insider.

Joyce told me to jump in her car and we'd head over. She and Dad and I all got free food, too. Joyce had pitched in when John was setting up his restaurant by giving him the money to get "his heart's desire" (as she put it) when it came to buying kitchen equipment. The agreement was that he'd pay her back sometime if the restaurant was a success, but when the restaurant succeeded beyond all expectations, Joyce said she didn't want her money back. Instead of repayment, John had framed one of his menus beside a certificate he'd made himself that read THIS ENTITLES JOYCE KUTSLOW AND DR. ROBERT NURSTROM TO FREE MEALS FOR ALL ETERNITY. John liked to be ceremonial. Dr. Nurstrom was Joyce's new husband — which still made me shudder a bit . . . invisibly, I hoped. Dr. Nurstrom had treated my dad.

We were heading off to the restaurant all the time, even on school nights. This evening, Joyce cleared off the passenger seat and then assembled herself in the driver's seat, making sure she didn't shut her pink flowered scarf or purple skirt in the car door. As she put on her purple-rimmed sunglasses with rhinestones, I wondered if there was a receipt in her pocket that said *Purple Sparkle Sunglasses.* Even though I felt the big gap between a little piece of paper and a whole person, I thought maybe receipts could paint a picture of someone like Joyce, with her big flowery clothes, pink purse, and bow-shaped rhinestone clips on her pink shoes.

"I have a surprise," Joyce announced as we started to drive.

"You do?" I asked. "So do I." Uh-oh, now I'd said it. Well, maybe I would go ahead and mention to Dad and his friends that I was maybe thinking of making a movie.

"You have a surprise, too!" she gushed. "Good, good, good. A beautiful late spring night, a happening restaurant, and two swinging chicks with secrets to tell!"

I watched the sky turn as pink as Joyce's shirt.

* * *

Phyllis and Dad were at their table in the corner. John's restaurant was so popular that his friends always took the least popular table as early as possible, to avoid the rush, or "mush," as we called it.

Phyllis had a pad of paper and a calculator along with her computer. Her legs stretched out from beneath the table, ankles crossed.

Dad jumped up and gave us a hug. Phyllis waved with a pencil in her hand and then kept punching in numbers.

Soon John came bursting through the swinging doors of the kitchen.

"Hail, hail, the gang's all here!" he cried.

And sure enough, I looked over and saw the last member of this gang, Carolyn, picking dead leaves off the potted plants that lined the walls and hung from the ceiling. I had mistaken her short, spiky red hair for another plant.

"Hey," she said in her low voice, raising a freckly, muscled arm. Carolyn worked at a gardening store where they allowed her to grow all the plants for John's restaurant. She tended the plants and had painted flowers and vines around the walls. For this, she, too, had earned the eternal free food certificate.

"Joyce, look at you! You match the evening sky!" John observed happily.

"And you match your kitchen!" Joyce squealed, pointing to his flour- and grease-smudged apron. I didn't know what made her so cheerful, her big secret or seeing John look so happy.

"Well, you are obviously busting out all over with this surprise of yours, Joyce," John said. "Carolyn, get your skinny behind over here so we can hear it. I gotta get back in the kitchen."

Carolyn came over in her own time, to show that no one could rush her.

Soon we were all seated and staring at Joyce. She looked nervous, which made me feel better that I was so nervous.

"Well, you know I'm married to a doctor," she began, "and so I have access to foolproof test results sooner than others. . . ."

"Oh my goodness! You were only married a few months ago!" John exclaimed.

"Joyce!" Phyllis cried. "I'm so happy!"

"You'll be great," Dad said quietly.

"She's pregnant," Carolyn explained to me in her flat voice. "I mean, that's what you mean, right?" I could tell she was very happy for Joyce, in her own unexcitable way.

After Joyce announced that, yes, she was ten weeks pregnant, she launched into the details of her wonderful doctor, who was not her husband since he wasn't the right kind of doctor. The ob-gyn was a woman Joyce really liked. Then she told us that she was planning to keep working almost all the way up to the birth and how she was only having a little morning sickness.

Phyllis calculated the baby's birth date — end of January — and John said he would make a celebration menu when she was ready to tell the world, since we were sworn to secrecy until she was three months pregnant. The menu would include baby peas, baby corn, baby carrots, and angel food cake.

"But right now, Mommy," John said, "I've got to get back in the furnace."

"Yeah, I've got to finish up and go," Carolyn said.

All for the best, I thought. I felt sad that I didn't have an opportunity to tell them about the movie, but I told myself that I was more relieved than anything else.

"Oh, wait a minute," Joyce called out as John and Carolyn started to leave. "Amalee's got a surprise, too. Don't you, Amalee?"

John turned, and Carolyn sat back down.

"Honey, do you have a surprise?" Dad asked.

"That's okay. Everyone's busy."

"Spit it out, Ama, honey," John encouraged. "I love surprises."

I tried to speak quickly.

"Thanks," I started, and then I *did* spit it out, starting with the two thousand eight hundred eighty-one dollars in the champagne bottle from my grandmother. There was a group gasp.

"She left all that to you in a bottle of coins?" Carolyn asked. "What a weirdo. Sorry — I know she was your grandmother. That's a ton of money."

Dad looked stunned. "It was a huge bottle," he murmured. "You haven't seen it. Wow. The coin bottle."

Phyllis's hand was still clapped over her mouth. I plowed on, including the idea I'd just had. "I'm going to make a film about endangered species and extinction. It will be short. It will be like one of those documentaries that Carolyn always takes us to at the movie place."

"Ha! I told you she wasn't asleep!" Carolyn said to Phyllis, who shrugged. I had caught Phyllis sleeping a few times when we went to see documentaries.

"And so," I continued, "I'll make a film that shows my . . . way of looking at things."

"Perspective," Phyllis broke in. "You want to make a

short film from your own perspective about endangered species. Somewhat scientific, but more personal. Right?"

"Yes," I said, exhaling. I'd spoken my mind without anyone telling me to stop. "I thought I'd get a digital movie camera — we had one we could use in my English class — and spend the summer doing this. I think this is the kind of thing I was supposed to do with the money," I added quickly, but I realized I didn't want to mention the note. "I mean, I guess."

How was everyone going to react? Twelve was feeling younger and younger.

"That makes sense. I can set you up with some film professors from my school," Dad said thoughtfully.

"If you don't mind restaurant leftovers, I can do your catering," John offered.

"Do you need a set designer, or do you want a natural setting?" Carolyn asked. "The owner of my nursery knows about endangered plants. Would that be helpful, or do you just want to focus on animals?"

I started to say that plants would be great, but Phyllis held up her hand. "Hold it, hold it," she ordered. And then she said the magic words: "Let's make a plan."

✿ CHAPTER FIVE ✿

The Wisdom of Frogs

Dad was in shock about my so-called inheritance. We were still at the restaurant, now eating dessert.

"How did you count all that money?" he asked finally. And before I could answer, he added, "I remember that bottle. I remember I joked that it was a lot like Sally's mom, larger than life and full of money."

Phyllis, Joyce, and Dad were at the table with me. Phyllis had put everything away and pulled a small calendar out of her purse. She'd also torn a few pages from her pad of paper.

"She went to the bank with that boy on your street," Joyce said.

Don't blush. Don't blush, I commanded myself. My face burned. "Kyle," I said, then quickly added, "and the woman at the bank, Ms. Hazlett, and Leslie Scott's mother helped me count it, too. We had those coin-counting machines."

"Almost three thousand dollars," Dad wondered out loud.

"You sure you don't want to save the money?" Joyce suggested.

"Sure, she's sure," Phyllis said, and Dad nodded. "Okay, let's go here. Budget. How much do you want to spend on it? I recommend spending less than the entire amount so you have a cushion if something unexpected happens."

An emerjunsee, I thought. Suddenly I thought I knew more about Sally than anyone at the table.

Phyllis looked at me. "Amalee?"

"Oh! Uh, two thousand dollars for the movie. That should leave plenty for any kind of emergency," I answered. Phyllis made a note.

"Timetable," she went on. "You want to wrap this up by the end of the summer, before school starts?"

"Yes," I said. "Let's say . . . August seventh, so that gives me some time to run over, right?" Phyllis nodded and made another note.

Joyce broke in. "How are you feeling about all this? Do you want it to be about all plants and animals? One species? One plant? What are your feelings here?"

"You mean, what are my emotions?" I teased. She couldn't be asking me that.

"That's *exactly* what I mean," she answered. "You have to have a passion about something in order to tell a story about it. What do you feel passionate about?"

I thought of Kyle. That would not be mentioned.

"Joyce is right," Phyllis said without looking up. She was making a list of things I'd need to get the project on its feet.

Phyllis was not a therapist, so maybe Joyce had more of a point than I'd thought. She looked up. Both women were staring at me now.

"Take your time, Amalee," Joyce said.

There was just the sound of clinking forks and glasses from the other tables. "It doesn't have to be in context. It can be anything you want to say," Joyce urged.

"She means it doesn't have to fit in with an overall picture," Phyllis explained. "You can just say an image."

"I'm thinking of some funny-looking little plant from a rain forest that can cure a disease, but we might never find it if we clear-cut the rain forests," I began.

"That's terrific," said Joyce. I didn't know why, though. "What else?"

"Well, then there's this other thing," I went on, trying not to think too hard.

Joyce had once given me a trick to help me survive seventh grade. Whenever I had to write a paper or give a report, she would say, "Just relax and speak." I would take a breath and say the assignment out loud and then give some idea of what I wanted to do with it. I always had to take a breath and let the idea out without getting too hung up on what I thought I should say.

So I relaxed and spoke.

"Who's to say we need a plant to cure a disease in order for it to . . ."

Silence.

"To what?" Joyce asked.

"To count? Why does it need to do something for *us* in order to count?"

Joyce's eyes welled up with tears. What had I said? She shook her head apologetically and explained, "It's the pregnancy. It makes me more emotional."

"Ah, so it's *the pregnancy* that does it," Phyllis said, winking at me. Joyce cried early and often, John always said, even when she wasn't pregnant.

"All right, all right," Joyce grumbled, dabbing her eyes. "Here's what I see. One point of your perspective is that we need to preserve species, because we need them for . . . medicine and . . ."

I thought about it for a second, then finished her

sentence. "For information, and for their beauty, and for that thing where everything eats something else and if we lose one thing, we lose many things . . . food chains!"

"Ah, yes, food chains," Phyllis said.

"But," I added, "that's not the whole thing, because even if a species is unimportant to us, it should survive. Because it just should!"

"Exactly. Those are the two halves," Joyce said. "On the one hand, we need them for our own survival. On the other, they have the right to be preserved from extinction even if we don't need them. That's what you're saying."

"Yes," I said. "Yes, those are the two halves. Is that a movie?"

Dad, who had been silent, leaned forward and added his voice to Phyllis and Joyce's. "That's a movie," he said.

"Yes, it is," Phyllis agreed.

And Joyce said, "Absolutely!"

Dad made a phone call when we got home from John & Friends. I started making the lists that Phyllis and Joyce had recommended. I wrote, *What We Need Animals For: Medicine, Food, Friendship, Clothes.* What else? Do we *need* them for beauty? I added *Beauty*. I went down the hall to ask my dad what he thought.

It turned out he was coming to find me. He held out the phone and said, "Here, honey, talk to Phil Novick."

"Who's Phil Novick?" I whispered.

"He's a film professor at NYU. He was one of my philosophy students."

"Dad!"

"Just talk with him. I told him you're looking for a camera, that's all."

"Hello?" I knew it was really nice of Dad to call a film professor, but I still felt nervous.

"Hey," Phil said loudly. "Making a film? What kind — fiction, documentary, animated, feature, short?"

"It's a short documentary about endangered species," I said. Where had I come up with this idea? Had my father taken me too seriously?

"Huh. Okay, what kind of effects are you looking at?"

"Effects?" I asked slowly.

"Yeah, yeah, special effects. For starters, do you need really clear sound or would you dub it later, adding sound to a big montage or something?" he reeled off.

"A montage . . ." I repeated, wishing I could run and look up *montage* before I answered.

"Yeah. Hey, how old are you?"

"Twelve." I stiffened. Would this end the phone call? But Phil didn't sound angry. "Ohhh, okay." He slowed down. "A montage is a series of images strung together to say something in pictures. Like in a movie when a couple is first dating, they play some rock song and show them sharing an ice-cream soda, then walking on the beach, then sitting by a roaring fire. . . . That's a montage."

"Oh, yeah, I think I've seen that movie," I said.

"There are about a million movies like that," he said, laughing.

"You forgot the scene with them walking a dog in the park," I pointed out.

"Hey, you're right! And also the newspapers over their heads in a rainstorm. Sounds like you're pretty savvy about these things. So, you got a piece of paper to write something down?"

I ran over to Dad's desk. "Yes." A film professor had called me savvy! I told him I wanted sound in the movie and also added to the movie, and that I wanted to put different bits of film side by side. He gave me the names of a few brands of cameras he'd recommend, what to ask for, and how much I should pay. He said I'd need a good computer to edit the film on (so cool! I heard this was how you edited movies now), and when the time came, he'd give me a short crash course.

"Good luck," he told me when we were done.

I brought the phone back to the cradle, but when I

went in to thank Dad, I found him just sitting on the couch in the living room, staring straight ahead.

When I sat next to him without speaking, he said, "I feel . . . I feel . . ." Poor Dad. Ever since he'd been sick, Joyce had forced him to describe his feelings. He'd had to confess how afraid he was of dying and letting me down and of being a bad friend. But really he just wasn't that kind of guy, so on a regular basis she'd ask him how he was feeling, and if he said, "Fine," he had to pay her a dollar, because she said that was too easy.

"Don't answer before you know exactly how you are feeling," she'd lecture him. "You're a human, not a machine that spits out the word *fine*." Even if Dad said he felt "content," he didn't have to pay a dollar. Just not "*fine*."

"I feel . . ." he now repeated, looking at the clock. Then he dropped his shoulders and gave up. "I can't believe she left that thing to you." Now he went and stood over the empty bottle. "Don't get me wrong — I'm thrilled that she gave you this money and excited about what you're going to do with it. But it's so strange for her, so out of character." He shook his head. "I only went there a few times. She didn't like me, you know."

No, I didn't know. I knew she didn't like him after they got married, but I didn't know she'd *always* disliked him. I sat completely still and hoped he would keep talking. His Sally stories reminded me of apple peels that you try to peel off in one long coil. If I interrupted or if he got distracted, he would change the subject, and I would only hear bits of information. It felt much better to get the long stories, the whole peel.

"I didn't go to the college she wanted me to go to, and Sally didn't, either. Sally was fun. She was smart, but she liked to have fun too much." What did that mean? I didn't ask. "Sally was great for me at first. I met her when I was hiking with Carolyn and Phyllis. We were hiking around, and we saw Sally and her friends. They asked where people went rock climbing. I pointed the way, and Phyllis said they would need the right equipment."

I noted to myself that Phyllis had always been Phyllis!

"Sally said something like 'How hard can it be to find a bunch of footholds and handholds?' And Phyllis got really prickly and asked how hard could it be to fall off a ninety-degree incline? After Sally left, Phyllis was either so angry or so scared for her that she made us go rent some equipment to bring over to your mom and her friends. By the time we got there, Sally and her friends were at the top of this rock face . . . so now Phyllis felt angry *and* humiliated." Dad started to laugh. "She was so angry! And Sally's friends looked as if they would have liked some of the equipment that Phyllis had brought, but Sally kept saying, 'I told you we'd be okay! I told you!' Phyllis stomped off, and we returned the stuff to the rental place. As we were leaving, Sally came running up to us and said, 'Don't be mad!' And she just draped her arms around our necks and kissed us both on the cheek and said, 'Peace! Peace! Are we friends? Are we?' I think Phyllis was even angrier, but I thought I was in love. And that's how it started."

I sat even more still, hoping that Dad would get lost in the story and keep going.

"It's funny," he said. "Now I teach kids who are that age. She was a certain type of person. You get one or two a year. They're the kind of people who act like trusting kids. You feel protective of them. You wince when they talk to strangers. I remember how easy it was for Sally to throw her arms around people she didn't know. And to climb up a cliff with no ropes or hooks or harness. Like a reckless, innocent child. I see those girls now. They are . . . in trouble. And then I see the nice, shy boys who try to protect them or even save them, and they . . . are in trouble, too."

I couldn't understand why the boys would be in trouble just for wanting to help, but Dad looked so upset when he was talking about it that I believed him. I could see him as one of those boys. He loved to help his friends. He must have *really* wanted to help Sally. And he must have been in misery when he couldn't help her. From all the things I'd pieced together, that seemed to be how the story went.

Dad looked away from the bottle and turned to me. "So, you really want to do this movie? Really?"

Agh, back to my life! I said yes and tried to sound like a responsible person with a plan. Or so I hoped.

"Then I'm going to help you get your act together. I have an exercise for you." He took me to his desk and cleared everything off except a few pieces of scrap paper.

"Make an outline," he told me.

"Yes, Professor Everly," I said.

"That's right," he answered. "I'll be like an advisor. College students have shown me how easy it is to lose your way if you don't get a good start. You're taking on a big project here! You know how you did props and lights for *Fiddler on the Roof* at school this year? Imagine you're doing props and lights and directing *and* writing."

"But I don't have to write any songs. And it's probably

only going to be about ten minutes long, so it's not as hard as writing a musical!" I protested, but that was just to buy some time. I was starting to panic. Who wouldn't?

"You sit and work on this for ninety minutes. That's nine-zero minutes, not nineteen."

I stared at the paper after Dad left. I wrote down the word *Dinosaurs* and thought about how I could start with a definition of extinction. The dictionary said extinction was "the death, destruction, or ceasing to exist of a species or family of organisms." Five minutes later, I had crossed out everything I had written, and I was bored. I wrote *Extinction and People*. Forget the dinosaurs. What did Joyce say my movie was about? *We need to save endangered species as a way to save ourselves, but also just because we should.* Right?

But how would I show that as a movie?

Maybe I'd start with a sick child in bed being cured by a plant from a rain forest that had been saved from logging. Hadn't I seen a movie like that? I thought of Phil Novick and me laughing about things we always saw in movies. I also thought of two girls I'd been not-really-friends with in the sixth grade, Ellen and Hallie. They had always been good at finding the most clever way to say a mean thing about a person. Now, in my head, they described the situation: *So let's get this straight. This is a movie that shows that you watch too much television and steal ideas from it.* I'd stopped being friends with Ellen and Hallie — or maybe they'd stopped being friends with me — but they still visited my mind from time to time when I was wearing pants that felt too tight or I had an idea that felt stupid.

So no sick kid on the bed. But then I had no ideas. I looked at the clock. I'd been sitting there for forty minutes. Not even half the time.

"Dad!" I called. "Any chance . . ." I thought maybe hot milk would help me relax and stay focused.

Dad stepped into the room as if he'd been waiting outside the whole time. "Congratulations. You lasted longer than most college students sitting down to write a paper. Now come with me."

"I'm not quitting," I explained, following him out the back door.

"Amalee," he said, as if he weren't listening, even though I'd learned a long time ago that he heard and remembered absolutely everything, "this is all part of the exercise. It's like the sound of one hand clapping."

"Oh, Dad," I groaned.

"According to some philosophies, if you listen for what one hand clapping would sound like, your mind opens up just in the attempt to think of the impossible."

"I can't understand what you're saying or why you're saying it," I said. "You're two for two."

"Here's the thing: I made you sit with an empty sheet of paper, trying to imagine something as impossible as hearing one hand clapping. I asked you to do something impossible." He led me out the back door to look at the woods.

"Thanks for your confidence in me," I murmured, looking at the wet trunks of the trees and seeing how green everything was after the rain.

"Oh, I have confidence in you, don't worry about that," Dad said, putting his arm around my shoulder. "But nobody can make an outline of a whole movie in one sitting. I was trying a writing trick on you. So now, take a breath."

"Who, me?"

"Yeah, take a breath." I took a breath. Dad said, "Just look and listen." We stood for a few minutes.

"What's that chirping sound?" I whispered. "Are those spring peepers?"

"Yeah. Remember those pajamas you had with frogs on them? You used to hop around in them and say you were a spring peeper."

After another minute, Dad added a suggestion. "One

important thing is to respect whatever pops into your mind."

The singing of the frogs was so dense, it sounded like a green curtain of sound hanging in the air of the woods. *Frogs, frogs*. My mind spun like the dial on a safe, trying to find the combination to open the door. There was something very beautiful about the frogs singing to us on a warm spring night. Like a Greek chorus, something we'd learned about in history. The Greek chorus was a part of ancient Greek plays. Even though it's called a chorus, it doesn't really sing. It's a group of people who all speak at the same time to comment about what's going on, talking about sad things and funny things and behavior that we all have but that gets us into big trouble inevitably, like the pride of a queen or the temper of a prince. And here were the frogs, in a world full of extinction, commenting to anyone who'd stop and listen. I suddenly remembered my grandmother telling me to watch and listen. This was spookily similar to what Dad was saying now. I kept listening. Some idea seemed to be at work here.

What had I heard about frogs? They were amphibians, so they were especially sensitive to the environment. Because they lived both on the land and in the water, the land and water both needed to be clean for them to survive. And then I thought about the tree frog I'd heard about whose skin was useful, because it was so poisonous that there were tribes who put it on the darts they used to hunt big animals. And there was a story about some kids in Minnesota who went on a school trip to a lake or a pond and found mutant frogs. Their discovery was the reason that all these studies started to happen, because what happened to the frogs was probably happening to humans, too.

Dad said that any idea that felt random but still wouldn't go away could be the key to everything. What could be sillier than the fate of the Earth sung to us by a Greek chorus of frogs? But the more I thought about it, frogs could tell the story of endangered species better than anyone.

I brushed past Dad to go inside.

"I've got to call Carolyn," I told him. "I've got an idea."

✿ CHAPTER SIX ✿

The Rain Forest in My Town

"I got you some chicken wire," Carolyn said, walking up our driveway the next day with the roll of wire fencing and a pair of clippers.

I had done what she'd told me to do after I'd shared my idea with her. I had laid out about ten newspapers and ripped up another twenty or so into two- or three-inch-wide strips. I'd also cut the top off an empty milk jug and filled it with a glue-and-water mixture.

"How big are these frog masks you want to make?" Carolyn asked as she inspected my preparations. I also had some pictures of frogs I'd printed out from Dad's computer.

"They should fit over someone's head," I told her.

"Whose head? Your age? Older?"

"I don't know," I admitted. "I haven't gotten that far yet."

Instead of throwing up her hands and leaving, Carolyn made a surprising suggestion.

"John told me he wants to be in the movie. How about him?" she asked. I had an image of John dressed all in green with the big mask on his head. He *had* to be a frog. But what if the other frogs were my age?

"He can be a bullfrog," I said.

Carolyn nodded without smiling. "Excellent choice for John. That would suit him. How many of these things do you want to make?"

"Three or four."

"You may want to call a couple of friends. This could take a while. Who's good at this kind of thing?"

I thought of my friend Marin. I hadn't seen her much during the year, but she'd helped make the sets for *Fiddler on the Roof*. When she and I had slept over at Sarah's, she'd sketched Sarah's little sister, Julie, and it was beautiful.

I called Sarah and Marin, and they both came over wearing old shorts and T-shirts, as I'd instructed. I looked up the street and decided I didn't have an excuse to call Kyle. He was a soccer player, not an artist.

Carolyn helped us mold the first frog head. She had

brought a book that showed frog masks from an island in the Pacific called Bali, and she had a book of animal masks from Mexico, too. Carolyn helped change the shape so our masks could fit over a whole head and still let a person breathe.

"We want to be frogs." Marin spoke for herself and Sarah when Carolyn asked who they thought should be the other frogs. Sarah nodded and laughed as she wrung the extra glue out of a newspaper strip.

"Okay," I said. "I think I need to tell you, though, that one of the frogs will have two heads. It's the frog that warns us about the pollution that affects them and could hurt us." I waited for Marin and Sarah to tell me that my idea was too gross, and that I was gross for even thinking it. In my mind, Ellen and Hallie were shaking their heads in disgust.

"Can I be that one?" Sarah asked. "I mean, unless you really want to be that one, Marin."

Marin shrugged. "That's okay. What's the other one?"

"You didn't tell me one of them had two heads," Carolyn muttered as she rifled through the pages of the mask book. "Let's see if there's something we can work with here. Do you want two whole heads side by side, or one head coming out where the ear hole should be?"

No one blinked. No one got grossed out. Sarah wanted

to be that frog. Sarah always surprised me. She was very pretty. She had reddish-brown hair that she said was "auburn." I loved this, because it sounded like oak leaves burning in the autumn, which really was the color of her hair. She wasn't skinny or fat — she just looked strong. She'd played the lead, a popular fifteen-year-old, in *Bye Bye Birdie* in the sixth grade, and she'd played Golde, a much older woman, in *Fiddler on the Roof* in seventh grade, and she seemed to like being Golde much better. She actually dyed big gray streaks into her hair a couple of weeks before the show. She also spent a long time talking with her grandma about coming over from Poland in the 1940s. She returned with perfect imitations of an older woman sighing, wringing her hands, and looking up and shaking her head at the sky. Every once in a while, she'd clutch her hip and say, "From my fall" — in her grandmother's voice, with her grandmother's shrug.

When she played Golde, she became a version of her grandmother. The audience loved every minute of it, and so did she.

I could never do that. I felt like I spent all my time trying to be pretty. To be un-pretty on purpose felt terrifying! And now Sarah wanted to be a frog with two heads. What would Kyle think? He'd probably think she was cool for not caring what other people thought. I felt a little envious of her bravery.

By the end of the afternoon, we had three papier-mâché masks: a big one for John, a small one for Marin, and a bigger one for Sarah that had two heads. Marin would be the tiny, colorful rain forest frog with the poisonous skin.

Marin said she would come the next day to paint the heads. I told her she could do anything she wanted. I trusted her. Carolyn didn't say anything. I could tell she was letting us run the show ourselves.

Dad got home from work and nodded at the unpainted heads. "Very nice!" he said. "But what's that?"

"That's the frog with two heads," Sarah explained, adding proudly, "that's mine."

I thanked Carolyn for her help.

"I wanted to do more," she admitted, "but this is your thing, I know." She took the almost-dry bullfrog head to fit it on John, promising to return it that night.

Dad took Marin, Sarah, and me out for pizza and then dropped them at home. Afterward, he surprised me by driving me up to Kingston, where we bought a great digital video camera, a tripod, a light reflector, headphones, and the microphone Phil had recommended. Phil said he would lend me another good one, too. The receipt said that the whole bill was one thousand two hundred fifty-eight dollars. In my head, I explained to my grandmother that this was what I really wanted to do, and I silently thanked her as I paid.

We came home to a message from John: "I can't wait to be a bullfrog. Does that mean I get to sing? Oh, please, oh, please?"

I woke to see my new camera on my desk. It looked like it had positioned itself with the lens pointing right at me, saying, *Go ahead and stand behind the camera, but you're the one in the spotlight.* I felt scared, singled out, spotted.

Marin was coming over at ten. I'd just spent over a thousand dollars on a camera and equipment. What had I gotten myself into?

I had a picture of myself as a filmmaking scientist that Kyle would think was really great. That was it. Wait — was that it? Was that the only reason I was doing this? I knew I wasn't like Sarah, who loved playing bizarre roles for the sake of playing them. I was afraid I was the opposite, a girl who did something just because I wanted a boy to like me.

The doorbell rang, and I heard the door open. It wasn't Marin.

"Ringie dingie, ringie dingie!" John sang from the hall.

And then I heard Dad greeting him, saying, "You shouldn't have!"

John answered, "How could I resist? Look at this broccoli!"

I sighed. Well, at least I had something to do to forget my sorry state of mind. I could go to the kitchen and let the world revolve around John's broccoli instead of Kyle.

The kitchen table looked like a full-grown garden. Besides the broccoli, which was a beautiful deep bluish-green, there was a big bundle of asparagus, a box with six baskets of strawberries, a huge bag of snowpeas, and a few heads of lettuce.

John was at our stove, pouring a bowlful of eggs into a frying pan.

"Frederick said he'd drop off my bags at the restaurant so I could come here. You should have seen what we got! I swear, that farmer's market is one of the best in the country. Even the yolks of these eggs are . . . did you see them, David? Is it me or are these the brightest orange yolks you've ever seen? And the asparagus — it's so tender! It's almost a shame to cook it. I'm going to braise it and serve it with some of these gorgeous fingerling potatoes and this wonderful steak that is so easy to cook, it practically does all the work for me. What is it that has made the Hudson Valley the Garden of Eden this year?"

"Maybe it's Frederick," Dad suggested. We'd certainly heard a lot this spring about Frederick, a new friend of John's who had his own restaurant in Woodstock. Dad winked at me.

"Oh, please, he's ten years younger than I am, first of all. Second, he's totally into fitness, while I don't fit into anything." John laughed at his own joke.

"What's braising?" I asked.

John spun around and looked at Dad, then me. "Did you know she was here?" he whispered.

"What's wrong?" I asked.

"Did you hear what I was talking about?" John asked.

"Honey, I think John's wondering if you knew he was gay," Dad said. Then he and I started to laugh.

"What?" John demanded, looking horrified. "Is being gay so funny? I knew I was gay when I was Ama's age, and I can tell you how funny it was *not* in Georgia. Not funny for me, not funny for my parents, or my church . . ."

Dad became serious. "I'm sorry, John," he said. Then he explained, "Amalee has known you were gay for a while now, and when we met Frederick and saw how he appreciated good food as much as you did, we made bets about how long it would take for you to go out on your first date."

John looked over at me. "And you were in on this?"

"I bet two dollars on Christmas," I confessed.

"Well, I never." John put down his spatula for a moment and covered his eyes. He shook his head. "How times have changed." Then he picked the spatula back up.

"And the location has changed," Dad pointed out. "And the friends."

"True, and I say hallelujah to that, can I have a witness?" John sprinkled some very wrinkly mushrooms on the eggs. "These mushrooms smelled so fresh, like rich dirt, like they'd just been picked in an enchanted forest. You just can't believe that they're from the same world as highways and airplanes and lawn mowers and all that . . . or are you going to say that's Frederick, too?" He stopped himself, looking over at us with a smile. He flipped the pile of steaming eggs onto a big plate and brought them over. "Ama, tell me about this movie!" he said as he served our eggs and poured some coffee for himself and Dad. "How did you get this idea?"

"Mr. Chapelle, my English teacher."

"I know Alex," John said.

"Well, he gave us an assignment to take a story off

the page in some way, and it was actually really fun. . . ."

I caught my breath and realized that Kyle was not a part of this story. Maybe I wasn't just doing this for him, after all.

I told them about Curt's opera about his mother and sister. I told them about my project, too.

"This sounds great, Ama," John said. "So you decided this movie would be another way to get the words off the page?"

"Yes, after seeing Mr. Chapelle's movie, it seemed like the best way. He made a movie about his son. Mr. Chapelle decided not to speak in the film, since he's an English teacher and feels like he's always getting up and explaining things, so he told the whole story without speaking."

"I'll have to ask him about that," John said, and Dad nodded.

Yes, it was Mr. Chapelle, not Kyle, who had inspired my wanting to make a film. When my grandmother had talked about how we lose things forever and lose the things they could teach us, I'd thought about the animals that were already extinct. Sarah had started that idea by comparing my grandmother to a great auk, but I had always, for some reason, been interested in endangered species and how weird it was that humans would let a plant or animal disappear completely.

The doorbell rang and Marin let herself in, lugging the books with frog pictures and the one with masks.

"Hi," she panted, putting a sheet of paper in front of me at the kitchen table. She had sketched frog heads with beautiful, bold colors.

"Look at that. I am one pretty frog," John murmured as he studied the pictures.

"Do you like them?" she asked.

"I can't believe you did all this work," I answered. "These are incredible." John and Dad agreed.

"Thanks," Marin said. "I'm ready to start."

John insisted that she have some eggs first.

"Protein sharpens your mind," he explained. Marin raved about the eggs and even said how great the mushrooms tasted.

"Enchanted, aren't they?" John asked, and Marin nodded.

"Oh, I came across a problem last night," Marin said later as she brought her empty plate to the sink. "I know you wanted to have a really beautiful tree frog, and you thought that it was the same frog they make the poison darts with, but the really poisonous frog is the golden poison frog. It's one of the most poisonous animals on the planet. So which one do you want, the really poisonous one or the really beautiful one?"

Whoops. When the haze of embarrassment had passed, I understood that Marin wasn't saying I'd been a fool. I realized she had just made something very clear to me: We needed both. We needed a beautiful frog *and* a frog that makes useful things for us. Each frog showed a different reason to protect a species. The bullfrog, I decided, would talk about food chains. The poison frog would talk about the important things we get from plants and animals. The two-headed frog would talk about how the pollution that affects them could be a sign of the pollution that affects us. But we needed a beautiful one, too. Yes! The beautiful one could stand for the fact that we love beautiful things and need to protect them. Then I felt sorry for unbeautiful animals. I realized we needed yet another frog. I'd call it Frog X. Frog X would be plain, unhelpful, and not part of any food chain that affects humans. We needed to protect Frog X just because. Because, because, because.

Marin then showed me a picture of a frog whose poison is used for a painkiller. She said in case I didn't want my medicine example to be a poison that's used to kill other animals, I could go with the frog whose skin made medicine. It was called a phantasmal frog, and it looked like a red and white peppermint.

I liked the golden frog better. "The tribe that uses the poison on darts to kill other animals —" I started.

"The Chaco tribe," Marin informed me.

"Cool!" I said approvingly. "The Chaco tribe uses the poison darts to kill animals they're going to eat. They don't make those animals extinct, and they don't kill the frogs in order to make the darts, right?"

"Right," Marin said. "I read about it. They wipe the darts on the frog's skin, and that's it. Gosh, imagine if you were in charge of doing that, and the frog jumped into your lap or something."

We both shuddered. "I want the golden poison frog," I told Marin.

"Yeah, I want it, too," Marin agreed.

Marin said she thought she could make more frogs without Carolyn's help. I started ripping the newspaper and mixing the glue.

As we constructed two frogs and painted five, I learned a lot about Marin. All I'd known about her family before was that they all had very dark brown straight hair, brown eyes, and pale skin. They seemed like they came out of the same fairy tale, like little royal shoemakers, even her parents. They were serious, but friendly and very polite. They even walked politely, and quickly. Marin now told me that her ten-year-old brother had already said he wanted to be "in finance," and that her mother had been pleased that he wanted to join her "religion." She was a banker. So was Marin's dad. That made Marin, who was every art teacher's favorite student, feel alone in her house. She said it wouldn't be so bad if her mother wasn't always mentioning that she herself was an artist whenever she decorated Christmas cookies or carved a jack-o'-lantern.

"I feel like she's saying, 'See, Marin? I like art, too, but I don't have to do it for a living! You can be a banker and *still* carve pumpkins.'"

I hoped Marin was wrong about her family. Anyone could tell that she loved to paint and make things. She was unstoppable.

"You are an artist," I said. "And you'll be an artist for a living. You love it and you're great at it."

In fact, I kept on getting hypnotized while I watched Marin work. For the golden poison dart frog, she painted a green circle for the eye and a pointy black oval for the pupil, and then she dabbed on some darker green — "just to give it depth," she said. Next she added a curved triangle with a greenish white to make it look reflective and then, with almost no effort, she drew a black circle around the eye and painted a line above it which brought out the squareness of the front of its head. He looked very angry and powerful, but then she painted a long line for his mouth that was slightly wavy and just a little goofy-looking, as if the frog was saying, *Hey, I didn't ask to have skin that could kill an antelope. Or, like, eighteen antelopes.*

Every line changed its personality. Then Marin took a sponge and blotted on a darker yellow paint than the one I had painted (I was allowed to do the first coat on each frog and that was it), and it went from a cartoony frog to a more realistic one. But it also looked like it belonged in an important ceremony, regal.

I murmured, "Amazing . . ."

Marin said, "Thanks." And she kept painting.

Marin broke one spell of silent concentration late on Sunday morning by saying, "So . . . your dad raised you, and Carolyn is his friend, and so is John from the restaurant, and Phyllis from school."

"That's right," I answered. "And they're also friends with Joyce, who's a therapist. She works with teenagers."

"I see. And I know your mom died," she continued quietly. "Is that hard for you?"

"No. My dad was already raising me when she died. I

mean, I feel sorry for her. She was kind of wild. I mean, she liked to do crazy things, like she was probably just driving too fast when she died. She was unlucky."

"So you know a lot about her?" Marin asked, continuing to paint the red-eyed frog's famous bulging red-orange eye.

"No, I don't," I said. I went through the short list in my head of what I knew about her. It felt funny to admit out loud to Marin how little I knew.

"Do you ask questions about her?"

"I think I want to," I answered. "But I don't want everyone thinking that I miss her. I don't want them to smother me and give me sad looks and get all serious about it."

"But you can tell them that, right? You can tell them you're just curious."

"It's so weird that you're talking about this," I said. "After my grandmother died, she left me this huge bottle of coins, but inside the bottle there was something really interesting. There were receipts for the last, like, forty years."

"Huh." Marin made a little grunt as she painted another frog's eye.

I started telling her what the receipts said, and how

they gave me little pictures of my mom. Marin was giving me her full attention now. She really looked interested.

"That's stuff most people don't know about their mothers who are alive!" she pointed out. "I don't know if my mom had sparkly barrettes."

"Well, the picture I have of my mom is that she has long, wavy hair and likes wearing sparkly stuff. But she's also a tomboy."

"Why a tomboy?"

"Because there was a receipt for boys' athletic socks and a basketball and a baseball cap," I said.

"Maybe it was for her . . ."

I stopped Marin and said, "She was an only child. She didn't have a brother."

"Oh." Marin pointed out that maybe she was just interested in sports but not a tomboy. True.

"And there was one from nineteen eighty-three for rubber bands for her braces, so I know she had braces."

"I don't know if either of my parents had braces," Marin pondered. "This is so cool. You know, your dad's friends are so nice. They would let you know more about her if you asked. They wouldn't think it was weird, I bet. You have these pictures, but they could tell you all the other stuff. You should totally ask. That's what I think, I mean." She looked embarrassed that maybe she'd said too much.

"Oh, I might!" I answered, trying to let her know I wasn't angry at her suggestion. I was just a little lost in thought. She was right, actually.

Just before Marin left on Sunday evening, Carolyn came by to see the masks.

"Wow," she said, unsmilingly focused on every detail. "You really lucked out, Amalee. This girl's got talent."

"Uh, thanks," Marin answered shyly, since Carolyn wasn't actually talking to her.

Carolyn looked straight at her now.

"Is this what you want to do? When you grow up, I mean."

"Yes. Absolutely," Marin answered.

"It's hard to make money," Carolyn warned.

"I can teach," Marin began quietly. "Or I can do graphic art. I'm already working with computers."

"You've thought about this," Carolyn observed. She raised her eyebrow, a sign of respect.

"Just as long as I don't have to combine painting with banking," Marin said, which confused Carolyn, but not me.

As Marin was leaving, I handed her an envelope I'd

gotten from my desk. In it was a ten, and two twenty-dollar bills.

"What's this?" she asked.

"Your payment," I said. "Fifty dollars." And before she could interrupt, I added, "Your work is valuable. It's worth money to me. You have to take it."

"Fifty dollars!" Marin gasped. "But it was fun!"

"Aren't we supposed to like our jobs?"

We both paused to imagine our different guidance counselors encouraging us to like our jobs. "My first paid work," Marin whispered. "That's really nice, Amalee." She left, holding the envelope away from her body a bit.

Carolyn asked if I wanted to talk with the owner of her nursery about endangered plants.

"I'd love that," I said.

She left when my dad came home from the dinner he'd had with some of his students. He liked to eat dinner with them every month or so, just to get them used to talking about philosophy and big ideas in a casual, social way.

I told him that since he'd done such a great job finding a movie camera whiz, I was wondering if he could help me find a person to talk with about endangered species, maybe someone at a zoo or an aquarium.

"An aquarium," Dad said. "Yes, I know someone at an aquarium. It's in Boston, but it's worth the trip."

"Could I take a train or bus there?"

"I could drive you there, but . . . we can work out the details if it comes to that." Dad went to his room and reemerged with a phone and a piece of scrap paper. He called information.

The next day, I called Henry Jeffers, a young biology professor who'd quit teaching to work for the aquarium a few years ago. I left a message on his voice mail and he called back a few minutes before I went to visit the nursery where Carolyn worked.

"Amalee," he said in a quiet, even voice, "this is Henry Jeffers returning your call."

"Thank you," I said, pressing my ear to the phone to hear him. "I don't know if you heard my message. I'm sorry I wasn't more specific. It's just that I'm making this movie, and I have five different reasons we should care about endangered species, narrated by five different frogs. That's as far as I've gotten, so I'm not sure what specific information I'm asking about, specifically."

There was a horrible silence on the end of the line. I shouldn't have said that to anyone but my diary or God. I felt so unprofessional.

"Well . . ." he started. Was he disappointed? ". . . If you want to know about endangered species, I think you've called the right place."

"Really? I was thinking if you could show me an example of something like the importance of food chains . . ." I rambled.

"How about an actual endangered species?"

"You have an animal from an endangered species there?"

"Yes, a very famous sea turtle named Myrtle, and she's very old. I am happy to introduce her to anyone who cares about her story. And she has some buddies here, too. Other endangered sea turtles."

Five minutes later, with my heart skipping beats, face flushed, and hands shaking, I finished writing down all the information. I would come out to Boston, to the New England Aquarium to meet a green turtle named Myrtle, as well as other sea turtles that the people at the aquarium were rehabilitating. Myrtle weighed seven hundred pounds and was over fifty years old. She had been at the aquarium since its beginning, longer than most of the staff.

As I pedaled past Kyle's house on my way to the plant nursery, I realized that I was more excited about old Myrtle than I was about him. No, not true. I was still more interested in Kyle. Where was he today?

I parked my bike at the store where Carolyn worked. On the way in, I took a very small pad of paper out of my pocket and checked the name Carolyn had given me.

"Is Betsy here?" I asked the girl at the cash register.

"Sure," she said. "She's restocking stuff at the back of the store. There she is."

I went back and saw Betsy, and I knew I liked her immediately. Her arms looked as strong and freckly as Carolyn's, except they were heavier and twenty years older. She had a white ponytail, a loose purple tank top, and a wristful of woven bracelets with little beads in them.

"Betsy?" I asked.

She grunted a yes as she heaved a bag of dirt onto its pile.

"I know Carolyn. I'm Amalee."

"AMA-lee." She groaned as she hoisted another bag. "Yes. Nice to meetcha."

"Do you think I can ask you some questions, and in exchange I can help you lift these?" I asked, nodding toward the wheelbarrow full of topsoil and mulch bags.

"Nah. Heavy lifting's good for me. But you can keep me company, and then I can show you some neat plants. Carolyn said you're making a film about endangered species."

"Yeah," I said, flipping open the notepad.

"You have questions for me? Shoot," she said. "I go to Ecuador every winter. Have been for eighteen years. I have seen species of plants that I think would have been extinct if they hadn't been brought back in captivity by friends of mine. It's amazing to see how fragile we are, as Sting says."

"I'm sure anything you can tell me would be perfect for my movie," I said, "if it has to do with endangered species." I explained how the movie was set up so far.

"Alrighty," said Betsy. "So you'll have these frogs giving us examples of these different aspects of the importance of the natural world. I got it. Good idea! I'm glad people your age are interested in this stuff," she continued, almost to herself. "It's important. I've seen it firsthand." She looked at the bags she still had to haul and then suddenly waved them off. "I want to show you something. A couple things." She nodded toward the back.

I pulled out the camera and asked if I could turn it on.

"Absa-toot-ly," she said. "I don't get any more presentable than this."

As we walked to a greenhouse, she told me that a quarter of the medicines we use come from the rain forest, at least originally. She said there were many rain forests, some of them in the United States as far up as the Pacific Northwest.

She led me into a tunnel-shaped greenhouse, then stopped in front of a row of white orchids and suggested where I should stand to show as many of them as I could. It all looked beautiful on camera. The art teachers were right when they said repetition was pleasing to the eye, and Betsy must have known this. She went into full expert mode as she stood in front of them, saying, "Most people think of the Amazon rain forest when they think of rain forests, and for good reason. There are thousands of species crammed into every acre. And we use a ton of different plants for our own purposes. There are things like wild yams, which are used for pain relievers and women's health in general, and then there's the annatto plant. You can get great red dye from the seeds instead of using chemical dyes. Some cosmetic companies are using annatto in their lipstick."

She went on to describe other plants, using long Latin names, that had been used in medicines and things that were used in everyday life. "It's endless," she said. "And don't get me started about the beauty of the rain forest. Obviously, that's another reason the Amazon rain forest is treasured. It's not just the beauty of each thing. It's how it all fits together. Stunning. Ingenious. No artist could have thought of it. We have great ideas. We have beautiful ideas. Nature is *the* greatest idea, in my humble opinion. Not that we can't love these plants one by one. Look at this." She pointed to a single orchid. "Bring your camera closer. This is the real movie star. Isn't that exquisite?" The camera allowed me to zoom closer and closer to the orchid. "This orchid was almost endangered. Humans were responsible for almost losing it, and my buddies, also humans, were responsible for bringing it back. I don't want people to feel like a bunch of reckless nature squashers, even though we can be. We are also able to repair our damage."

She took me to another greenhouse to film her showing me the wild yam plant and some other orchids. After our interview, she took me back to her office.

"Here," she said, pulling down a bright yellow coffee can. She fished around and pulled out a woven bracelet. "They make these in Ecuador. These brown things are seeds from the tangua tree. Girls around your age sell them for about twenty-five cents. Every time I go down there I buy about fifty, and I get about fifty smiles. I'm a sucker for a smile. Do you smile?"

"Me? Sure I do!" I answered. "I guess I'm just nervous right now. I said I was going to make this movie, and everyone believed me so quickly. I'm not sure I know what I'm doing."

"Well, I'll tell you, eighteen years ago, I wasn't sure I

could ride in a hollowed-out tree trunk down the Amazon, but you know, I just jumped in, and here I am to tell the tale. So I must have known something." She tied the bracelet around my wrist. "This is for a fellow adventurer and planetary healer. Welcome to the club."

I admired my bracelet as I biked home. I also thought about Sally. Betsy had done crazy things just like Sally. Betsy had gone down to other countries and had become part of a North and South American Ecuadorian rain forest alliance. She had survived this big adventure she had taken. Would Sally have been like Betsy if she had survived, frazzle-haired but still an actual, responsible grown-up?

I noticed Kyle's car in his driveway as I went by, and I straightened my back, as if he was watching and actually noticing my posture. When I got home, I took in the mail, and there was an envelope that said *Amalee* with no address. It was a girl's handwriting, I noticed, dismissing the crazy idea that it could be from Kyle.

I dropped the other letters on the front table, where there was a note from Dad saying that Joyce would be happy to take me to the aquarium the next day. Henry Jeffers had called to say he could see me anytime in the afternoon.

Excellent news. Again, I imagined mentioning to Kyle

that I was doing some research at the aquarium. I opened the envelope and unfolded a picture by Marin. It was a watercolor of a pretty teenager with braces, wavy hair, red sparkling barrettes, white socks, pink sneakers, and a pink T-shirt that said MYSTERY GIRL. At the bottom, Marin wrote, *Your mom! I didn't have a picture, so I made her look like you.* My eyes shot up as I saw the small nose and eyes and the wide smile. My mother, who looked like me.

I decided that when I set out with Joyce for the aquarium the next day, I would get Henry to tell me about Myrtle the sea turtle, and Joyce to tell me more about Sally.

✿ CHAPTER SEVEN ✿

The Myrtle and the Mother

Joyce started to knock on the screen door, then just shouted as she let herself in, "Yoo-hoo! Is there a film-maker in residence?"

"Not yet," I groaned, double-checking my canvas bag for my camera, film, money, notepad, tape recorder, and lunch. Did I have everything? Tripod! I grabbed the tri-pod out of the closet.

"Not yet a filmmaker, or not yet ready to leave because you haven't had your coffee yet?" Joyce asked, laughing. "Just kidding about the coffee. Wait a few years for that." She wandered into the kitchen and poured herself some lemonade. Then we headed to the car. "Hey, you notice my safari outfit?" She was wearing light canvas sneak-ers and khaki shorts with lots of pockets. And she had on a pink shirt with lace around the sleeves.

"Your shorts say 'safari', but your shirt says 'meeting the girls for lunch'," I told her.

"Well, perfect," she answered, "because today I'm doing both, smarty-pants." As we put on our seat belts in the car, she said, "You know, people tell me I'm awfully calm for a mother-to-be, but I explain that I've helped raise a child before, and I've even managed to be friends with a preadolescent. Then they understand."

We were ten miles into the trip when I found a good time to look at the dashboard and ask, "Was my mother as wild as Phyllis and Carolyn say?"

"Ummm, yeah, pretty much," Joyce said, not sounding overly sympathetic or even surprised. It seemed like a good start. "In a very sweet, loving way. She was like a child, and people liked her, so she got away with it."

"She didn't get away with it with Phyllis," I pointed out.

"That's true. She annoyed Phyllis. Well, to be entirely truthful, her behavior *was* exasperating sometimes, especially if you believe that everybody has to grow up eventually and learn how to do the laundry and cook and clean. If you don't, that means somebody else is doing it for you." Joyce was reasoning it out to herself now, it seemed. "It's important to keep your childlike self alive, but she was more like an actual child, and your dad didn't mind cleaning up after her."

"He did her laundry?"

"Yes, he did most of the housework, but he also talked with their boss — they worked at the same restaurant — when she kept being late, and convinced the boss not to fire her. Before you were born, he would try to get the shift before hers so if she was late, he could cover for her."

"Why?" I felt like I could ask this without Joyce clamming up. I would never ask my dad something so out-in-the-open curious.

"Well, there are words for it in psychotherapy. I think he believed she wasn't capable of changing. I'm guessing that he wanted to protect her from finding out how weak her weak spots were."

"He felt bad for her?"

"He protected her as if she was fragile."

"It sounds like she *was* fragile," I said.

"I'd say no, and yes, and hmm . . ." Joyce thought out loud again. "Yes, she was fragile like a child. She had big butterflies on her shirts, and there was this way she opened her eyes very wide when you talked to her, because she thought everything was fascinating and wonderful. But no, she wasn't fragile, because she went to college for two years, she loved to read, and she was perfectly capable of acting like an adult if she wanted to. So, in a way, she wasn't doing the work you need to do to grow up, and she needed to. If you're late, you get fired. If you don't do the laundry, you wear dirty clothes. I felt sorry for her, since no one was there when she was growing up to notice her success or help her past her failures. Her parents were older when they had her . . . well, my age, actually, but I'm much hipper." She thought about this for a minute.

"You are definitely more cool," I agreed, hoping she would get back to Sally.

"Yeah," she murmured as she returned to the story. "Sally's father was a very busy guy, an international banker. He was basically never home. And her mother was just angry."

"Angry at what?"

"There are big therapy words for her, too, but basically she had big ideas about her own importance, but they didn't match reality. She was very smart, graduated with all sorts of honors from college. Sally called them fancy prizes. So she had all these fancy prizes and not much to do with them. She was interested in music and — what was it? — chemistry. No, biology. She once told Sally she'd wanted to be a marine biologist."

I imagined a woman who looked like Betsy from the

plant nursery standing knee-deep in ocean water, sunburned shoulders, hair blowing in the wind. Not my grandmother.

"Hey, what a coincidence!" Joyce exclaimed, giving me a jolt. "You're a bit like her, aren't you? Look where we're heading! By the way, do you have questions for this man we're going to see?"

I decided I'd learned as much as I could about Sally without opening the box of Joyce's therapy questions about how I felt hearing all this information. I knew how I felt. I loved hearing it, even though it felt a little funny to hear she could be "exasperating."

"I have questions for Mr. Jeffers," I said. "But hopefully he'll just want to talk about Myrtle."

"Myrtle the turtle?"

"Yeah. He says her name like she's his girlfriend."

"That sounds suspiciously like a stereotype about scientists," Joyce objected. "Just because they love their work doesn't mean they confuse their passion for science with their ability to have a social life. Look at Robert. Before he and I were together, everyone thought he was all about work."

Ah, *that* was why Joyce was touchy. I still refused to call her husband Robert. He was still Dr. Nurstrom to me.

Joyce had a point about him, though: Before she swept into his life with her lavender perfume and rose-colored scarves (not to mention her rose perfume and lavender-colored scarves), his biggest love outside of medicine seemed to have been jogging and looking nervous. Joyce saw something we hadn't seen. He even wore a pink tie at their wedding.

"You know," she went on, not looking in my direction, "if you start dating someone, you could always talk to me about it. Therapists are very good at respecting privacy." She whispered the word *privacy*. I said nothing. Phyllis had made the same offer while drilling me on geography, out of the blue explaining that school employees were bound by confidentiality rules. And Carolyn had said, simply, "Nothing shocks me. And I can keep a secret."

It felt right to tell no one about Kyle. I didn't have the urge to tell anyone. Joyce jumped into the silence of the car and said, "Rest stop! Time for a rest stop!"

We got to the aquarium by twelve thirty, after four rest stops. Joyce called Henry Jeffers from her cell phone when we were a mile away, and he was waiting for us at the main entrance. He had said he was "a tall black man in a red plaid shirt." He looked about ten years older than my dad's students.

“You look like you’re shooting a film!” he said, seeing my camera bag. Actually, it was an old canvas bag with lots of outside pockets that I’d found in the hall closet, only to find out later that it had once been used as my diaper bag. I blurted this out.

He laughed and said, “Maybe you’ll start a trend. C’mon in. I’ll introduce you to some of the sea life, and then you can meet Myrtle.” He flashed his pass in front and brought us in for free, which made the whole thing feel official.

The first thing I saw in the dark aquarium was a beach party of penguins. I almost didn’t see the glassed-in rail that held them, so they looked like they were just hanging out. Beyond them was obviously the main attraction of the aquarium, the three-story tank with a ramp spiraling all the way up to the top.

Henry could tell from how still I was standing that I’d never been here before. He told me this was called the Giant Ocean Tank.

“Pretty awesome, huh?” he asked.

He identified some of the fish for me. “Those ones with the low eyes that look like they’re up to no good, those are called permits. And there’s a moray eel. And a southern stingray. Sand tiger shark . . .”

“Shark?” I asked.

"Uh-huh. They don't attack the other fish or the divers."

"You have people diving down into this tank?" I asked. Then I felt embarrassed. I could just feel Joyce looking pleased at my excitement.

"Would you like to see some rain forest frogs?" Henry asked.

"You have frogs here?"

"Yes, when you said the frogs would be narrating the movie, I forgot to tell you we have some here. They're exquisite."

He was right. They were extraordinary, super-small frogs from Central and South America, like swirly, poisonous gumdrops. We'd passed some sea tanks on the way to the frogs' terrarium. They, too, were all works of art. Henry talked about the different worlds in the reefs off of Australia and Asia, going too quickly for me to turn this into an example of a food chain. If nothing else, I could see how each tank really was like a separate planet. I also laughed when I saw a piranha, one of the world's most dangerous fish, in its own dark tank as if it had been put there on a permanent time-out. "I'd love to see *that* guy at feeding time," I muttered.

Henry said the frogs lost their toxicity in captivity, but that the aquarium had lots of information about the different uses for the poison on their skins. During one pause, as we were admiring a bright blue and black frog, Henry said, "Want to see Myrtle now?"

Henry led me to one of her favorite spots, around the ledges at the bottom of the giant ocean tank. A school of fish caught my eye, but Henry tapped my shoulder and pointed. Joyce and I both gasped. A giant turtle took up most of the view. She swam placidly past the fish, almost nodding to them politely. Then she parked her head between two rocks as if she was trying to hide. I could spend an afternoon just admiring her rough, pebbly, webbed foot slowly waving behind her.

"That's my girl," Henry said, then pointed up to a diver who was descending with a late lunch, I guessed, for the sea creatures. I had been filming Myrtle for a few minutes (it took a while to remember to get the camera out), and I watched as Myrtle backed out of the rocks and joined the party. The diver was looking at the other fish, but when Myrtle emerged, he stroked her back with his flipper. I could do that for a living, feed the fish and pet sea turtles with my foot. A minute later, Myrtle decided to take a trip to the top of the tank. Her feet rippled in the water and she seemed weightless as she swam, belly to us, up past her younger friends (including the diver, who was probably half her age). Finally, I turned off the camera and asked if we could go to a place where I could film Henry answering the questions I'd brought.

Henry looked at the camera, surprised. "Sure," he answered nervously. He stepped away off of the ramp so people could get by. "How's this? Enough light?"

I noticed that when he stood near the big tank, he had a watery green ripple pattern on half his face. I liked the color but not the blotchiness. Joyce agreed to hold the reflective silver fabric to catch some more light and bounce it onto his face, and it worked perfectly.

"What would you say is one of the most important reasons to protect endangered species?" I asked first.

"Well, our survival depends on the survival of all the other species on the planet. I guess that's the number one reason . . . but I think, for me, I just want to live in a world with an infinite variety of flora and fauna — and rocks, for that matter. I want to be on a planet with countless life-forms. What would happen in a world without sea turtles? Myrtle swims up and down in the tank like a prehistoric angel," he said, swishing the air with his hands to demonstrate. "And their carapaces, their shells, look like ancient mountain ranges. I think that's one of the reasons so many mythologies say the Earth is actually the back of a great big mother turtle. Don't get me wrong — there are many ways in which sea turtles are essential to the health and vitality of the planet. But they're also just amazing. I want animals like sea turtles to be here on the planet, where they belong."

Suddenly Henry looked down. Then he looked up and said, "Okay, take two! Sorry. Do you want to erase that?"

I was dumbstruck. I loved what he had said. Joyce put down the silver reflector to dab her eyes.

"Allergies," she lied, blowing her nose.

I said, "It's digital. You can just keep going."

"All right." Henry cleared his throat. "Look at all the things we can learn from sea turtles. Not only do they form an essential link in a food chain that runs from plankton to humans, we can also use their movement as a model for our own aquatic locomotion, we can synthesize materials inspired by the leathery skin on their carapaces, and we can even learn about climate change from alterations in their migrations. The most important reason we should be concerned about extinction is that we're only scratching the surface of what we can learn from every species. If they disappear, who knows what may disappear with them? That's it." Henry looked happy and relieved to be finished.

"And that was perfect," I told him. "Very helpful."

"Thanks," he said. "Usually, Myrtle gets all the camera time. I was a little nervous. Did my shirt look right?

Oh, gosh, I could have worn a T-shirt from the endangered sea turtle project. It had a Web site."

"We couldn't have read it," I assured him. Was this the same quiet guy who'd called me up a week ago? "What you did was really, really good."

Joyce said, "She's right. Really, really good." She gave him a smile and a thumbs-up.

I pulled out the permission slip for Henry to sign for himself and Myrtle. "Let me know when it's done," he said. "My fiancée and I would love to see it."

Joyce raised an eyebrow at me.

Henry took us farther up the ramp before we left. "In the late fall, there are always cold-shocked sea turtles that end up on the shores of Cape Cod. The Audubon Society hosts the volunteers who bring them to the aquarium for rehabilitation."

"Volunteers bring them here?" I asked. "How?"

"In their cars. And the sea turtles can't get too warm too quickly, so people can't turn the heat on. That's pretty cold for driving around New England at Thanksgiving."

"It would be worth it to ride around with a sea turtle," I said. "Even if it smelled, too."

"Oh, I believe it does," Henry agreed, "But I agree, it would be worth it to save one of these . . ." He pointed to a smaller sea turtle swimming around with the fish.

"We've had to hold onto this one. He's not quite rehabilitated yet. But he is the most endangered sea turtle in the world, a Kemp's ridley." That straightened my back a bit. What if I was the person who'd picked up a sea turtle on the beach, only to find out that if we didn't save these animals one by one, there would be, as the definition of extinction said, a *ceasing to exist* of the turtle I held in my hands?

After loading me up with booklets and papers to read, Henry walked us to the entrance. Joyce and I waved good-bye and went to the car.

"Aquatic locomotion!" Joyce snorted as she turned on the ignition. "I hope you didn't erase the good stuff he said."

"No, no. I got it. That was awesome, how much he cares about it."

"Yes, it was. Amalee, I think you're onto something."

I was beginning to think the same thing. Not because I was asking such great questions. It's just that I was getting such great answers.

✿ CHAPTER EIGHT ✿

Hope Takes a Belly Dive

So now I had interviews with Betsy and Henry. What next? I decided to find out more about the deformed frogs from Minnesota that had made me want to use the two-headed frog narrator. I called the University of Minnesota and then the Minnesota Pollution Control Agency, and finally the North American Amphibian Monitoring Program. Everyone said they'd send pictures and some basic information if I sent a formal request. When I told the woman at the monitoring program that I was twelve, she said the kids who had originally found the mutated frogs were around my age. They'd gone off on a field trip and found one mutated frog after another; scientists were still trying to figure out what chemical was responsible.

When I got off the phone, I wrote three quick letters

and put them in envelopes before I forgot to do it. I brought the letters out to the mailbox.

Kyle was washing his car. Before I could stop myself, I walked down the street to his driveway. "You need some help?" I asked. "I owe you a favor."

"Oh, hi, Amalee," he said, and turned off the hose. "I'm fine. I'm almost done."

He wasn't wearing a shirt. And his underwear was coming up from under his saggy pants. It was a good look for him.

"Hey, are you making that film?" he asked.

"Yes, I am," I said as breezily as I could.

"Cool. Is it almost done?"

My ego shut down like a big machine unplugged from its socket. "No, not yet. I have the outline of it, and I've spoken with a marine biologist and a botanist. So it's coming together."

"I'd say," Kyle agreed. "Let me know if you need some help." He smiled. "You know, heavy lifting or something big dumb guys can do."

I looked at his dripping car for a few seconds and said, "You're not dumb," which, out loud, sounded really dumb.

"Thanks," he said, laughing. He turned the hose back on and started spraying the bumper. I waved and took off a little too fast.

The phone rang as I came inside, the screen door banging behind me. It was Sarah, inviting me to go swimming. "Take a day off!" she shouted into the phone.

I decided to take the day off since there was no way I could think of to turn it on.

While I waited for her stepmom to pick me up, I looked at my camera bag and decided to bring my camera with me. I put it in a plastic bag and put the whole thing in the canvas bag. There was enough space to fit my swimming things, too.

Sarah and her stepmom, Lydia, showed up twenty minutes later while I was reading the sea turtle articles that Henry had given me. A few things were becoming clear as I read. One was that species don't need just one or two things to survive. They need the right ecosystem with all the right conditions, the right things to eat, the right things to eat *them* to control their population, the right climate, enough space to stretch out and go where they need to go without going through places where they'd be killed, and, of course, clean water and clean air. It was like a perfect and complicated fabric, and I couldn't imagine talking about all of it in a short movie. I could cover only the tiniest thread. But I also wanted to know more. This was the kind of thing I wanted to study.

As we drove to the swimming hole, I saw the ecosystem

of our woods, with moss along the trunks of some trees and ancient, knotty bark on others, some with giant floppy leaves and others with long needles spiraling all the way to a distant point. I thought about Betsy telling me there was a mathematical order to how things grow so that even when things looked wild, there was a natural design that made sense to the eye.

Lydia and Sarah wanted to know more about my interviews so far.

Sarah asked, "Do you have anything for the two-headed frog to talk about yet?"

I said not exactly, but that Betsy and Henry had both said things I might use.

"Let me know if I can help," Lydia joined in. "I have a few skills. I can drive, for instance." It always took me a few seconds to figure out when Lydia was joking. She had the tightest ponytail I'd ever seen, but she had a very loose, funny personality.

"She's a great swimmer, too," Sarah added, laughing.

After about an hour of swimming, which included about fifty cannonball jumps off the high ledge, I climbed onto the shore and stared at the sand, the grass, and the ants. I filmed them in their tiny ecosystem, even though I wasn't sure I would find a place for them in the movie.

Then I filmed Sarah and Lydia, just because they looked so happy swimming and jumping. Sarah burst above the surface at one point and swam right up to the camera.

"I am Sarah Smythe. Remember who I am when you are a famous filmmaker!" Through the camera lens, I could see the sun glinting off the drops on her eyelashes and making her eyes sparkle. I told her she looked like a movie star, and she groaned and said she would splash me if I didn't have my camera.

On the way home, we passed Kyle's house. He was mowing his lawn with the same no-shirt, cutoff shorts, and underwear ensemble.

"Oo-la-la, who's that?" Sarah asked, pressing her finger up to the window.

"That's . . . that's just my neighbor, Kyle."

"What a god!" she gushed, hardly listening.

I sank into my seat, and so did my heart. If I was a guy and I had to choose between me and Sarah, I'd choose Sarah. She had made herself unpopular in our class by doing things like putting those gray streaks in her hair, but that was probably the kind of thing a high school guy would love, especially someone like Kyle who liked smart girls. She was smart and brave and beautiful.

"Uh, a little old for you," Lydia pointed out quickly.

"And if you disagree with me, we're going to lock you up like Rapunzel in a castle turret and shave your head every week, just in case."

"I can look," Sarah protested.

"No, you can't," Lydia answered. Then she joked with Sarah by saying something that hit hard for me. "You should be like Amalee. Think about endangered plants and turtles."

Well, at least they hadn't guessed how I felt about Kyle. Still, I felt like a big nerd. No, not a big one — a small, invisible one.

When I got home, I looked out the window once and saw Kyle pushing the lawn mower into his garage. Then I went to the bathroom and looked in the mirror. Pale, with a very plain face, eyes too small, ears too long, nose . . .

"Amalee?" Joyce was calling from the front of the house.

I ran out to find her before she discovered me examining my features.

"How did it all turn out?" she asked excitedly. I frowned. "The film! How did the footage come out?"

"Oh. It came out fine," I answered.

"Amalee, are you okay? Were you sleeping?"

"No, I was just looking at something," I said. "Can I ask you something?"

"Anything. You know that," Joyce said with the kind of eagerness that made me feel uncomfortable.

How could I begin to ask if I was the dullest-looking girl in the world? "How does a person . . . get a style?" I asked. What had I just asked? But Joyce launched right in.

"A very interesting question!" she chirped away. "Well, the best way to do it is to just pick up whatever you love. I love pinks, purples, soft fabrics, summer flowers, a little bit of sparkle and shimmer, and, *voilà*, I think that's what you'd say is my style, but it's really just, well, stuff I like."

"Do I have a style?" I asked quietly.

"Why, yes, you do. It's classic. You tend to go for simple things in blues and greens, and you choose things that make the most of your lovely features!"

"I don't have lovely features," I murmured.

"What? You're pretty and you have poise. Do you know what that means? It's one of the best kinds of beauty. It means that you hold your head up straight and look like you have a sense of purpose. It means you have presence," she gushed. "Oh, honey, are you worried about your style?"

"Oh, no, I . . . was just wondering."

"Okay," she said. "Okay. But when I was walking with you into the aquarium, and you were wearing that blue tank top that goes with your eyes, and you had that cool camera bag slung over your shoulder — it doesn't look like a diaper bag — I thought you looked very well put together. And I wanted to ask where you got those cool sandals that go up over your ankles."

I thought I might begin to cry, even though that was usually Joyce's department. Luckily she didn't notice, or she would have wanted me to explore my feelings. But I was feeling better. Seeing Sarah look at Kyle felt like getting a poisonous snakebite, and Joyce had just swept in on a vine to bring me the antidote.

Joyce was already getting herself a glass of water and asking every question she'd thought of in the car. Who would be the fourth and fifth frogs? Had I started writing a script? Was I getting the information I needed? I felt a little panicked. No, I said, I hadn't come up with people for the fourth and fifth frogs, but I was working on it. The truth was that I didn't want Joyce to volunteer. One big frog was enough.

I told her I was starting to fill in information for each of the frogs. So far, I had something for every one except for Frog X, the frog who we save from extinction for the sake of preserving all species from our harm.

"Well, Henry's impassioned speech about all the colors and uniqueness of all species, that's a defense of Frog X, don't you think?" Joyce asked.

"I'll write that down," I said, pulling my tattered notepad out of the camera bag.

"Is that all you have to keep track of everything?" Joyce asked disapprovingly.

"Uh . . ."

"When you undertake a creative project, you need SPACE!" Joyce cried. "You've got to get big markers in different colors and a big pad of paper to write it on."

The great thing about the summer is that one minute you're talking about something, the next, you've written a quick note to your dad and you're off in the car, heading to the art store to get a big pad of paper and lots of different colored markers. And on your way home, when it's summer, and when the driver of the car is pregnant, you have ice cream for dinner.

It was after seven o'clock when we drove home. I stared out at the trees and fields. The sun was undertaking its creative project by filling up every space with pink and gold light. Suddenly I saw what I thought were four scarecrows, but they were all moving in a slow, almost eerie way. I gasped. "What's that?" I asked.

"Oh, those are the tai chi people," Joyce said, as if

they were something you'd see at a zoo. "You've never seen them before?"

They were slowly raising their elbows with their hands hanging down, and at the same time raising one knee.

"Are they imitating flamingos?"

"No, I believe they're imitating cranes," she said. "They also imitate other animals. They're sort of channeling the energies of different animals."

"Do you think I could talk to them about . . . about the film?" I asked shyly. I heard my old friend Hallie saying, with quiet disapproval, *Not everything is about your little movie.*

"Let's ask," Joyce answered, nodding to point out that they were finished for the night. Without waiting for me, she peeled off to the side of the road, arranged her skirt and shirt, and got out of the car.

The tai chi people, as she'd called them, were quietly dabbing themselves off with towels that had been draped over a wooden fence near their cars. A man with curly brown hair and a nice smile looked right up at us as we approached. No turning back.

"Greetings," he said.

I assumed they didn't want any sudden jerky movements or loud voices, considering how slowly they'd been doing their dance.

"Hi," I said quietly. "My name is Amalee Everly, and I'm doing a film about endangered species. I was wondering if I could talk to you about the animals you imitate with your tai chi."

"Sure," the man said. "We can talk about that."

"I would want to film you. Would that be all right?" I added. By now, the three other people, all wearing baggy shirts over leggings, were leaning over in my direction like fascinated giraffes. Did they imitate giraffes, too?

The man turned to the other tai chi people. "It's fine with me. Is that okay with you?"

The other people nodded and murmured.

"Is this a movie for school?" the man asked.

"No, I just wanted to make a movie. I inherited my grandmother's coin bottle, and there was enough money to make a movie."

One of the women spoke. "Lucky you. My grandmother collected string."

We all laughed — quietly, of course. Kevin said to come by any night, and Joyce made me promise to come back soon. She said she had a feeling in her gut that this would be a good interview. She pointed to her pregnant belly and said, "And that means there's two of us that think so."

✿ CHAPTER NINE ✿

Monkeys

Dad was home when Joyce drove me up, so both of them helped me come up with lists. Joyce was right about going to the art store — it felt great to spread out. We'd bought a pad of paper that came up to my waist. Since we were still feeling guilty from the lecture Henry had given us about human garbage and the destruction of habitat, not to mention pollution, we got one hundred percent recycled paper and nontoxic markers.

"Beyond that," Joyce had warned, "I don't want you worrying about wasting paper. You might need a lot of it to map out the big picture, pun intended!"

Now I was working on "the big picture," with two pages for each frog.

On the *Pollution Warnings* page, though, I only had the deformed Minnesota frogs.

For *Beauty* I had Betsy's plants and the fish Henry had shown me at the aquarium before he'd introduced me to Myrtle and the other sea turtles.

For *Usefulness, Including Medicine* I put tai chi and Henry's comments about ideas for technology coming from sea turtles. In the back of my mind, I thought of Mr. Chapelle's son communicating with dolphins, but that seemed so private. I wasn't sure if I wanted to use him as an example.

Food Chains and *Frog X* were both empty. Dad suggested that I also call food chains *The Web of Life* so I wouldn't limit my thinking to an actual chain. He was right. An ecosystem was all interconnected, not just an up-and-down ladder.

"I haven't gotten very far," I pointed out.

"What kind of people would you like to talk with next?" Dad asked. "If you could talk with anyone?"

"Good question," I thought out loud. "A person who makes medicine that comes from plants or came from plants originally, a person who studies 'the Web of Life,' if there is that kind of person, someone who works at a zoo . . . that's all I can think of."

"That's a good start," Dad said as Joyce nodded. "I have an idea. What about the biodiversity wing at the Museum of Natural History? Biodiversity is all about having a wide range of species and what we need to do to preserve diverse ecosystems. An ecosystem is —"

"I know what an ecosystem is," I said, pretending to be very bored. Then I smiled. "I found out yesterday."

"That's a pretty big concept. Did you get it?" Dad asked.

"Got it and loved it," I answered.

Joyce laughed and then ducked out to make dinner for her husband. "And a second dinner for me," she added, winking at me.

Before I went to bed, I looked at myself again. I didn't look so bad. Then I saw Marin's drawing of my mom. The hair clips and the sneakers. Did she want to sparkle so she wouldn't look like a boy? Did she like the combination of rhinestones and gym shorts? There weren't a lot of pictures of her, but come to think of it, I looked like her. And I'd always thought she was beautiful.

I woke up feeling better about everything, which was fortunate, because Sarah came by unannounced while I was having breakfast.

We sat out on the lawn to eat some fresh peaches that John had brought by. "My mom and I were just at my sister's dance class," Sarah said. Lydia had dropped her off while she did errands. "I want you to come with us when we go pick my sister up. I told the teacher about your film, and she said I gave her a brainstorm. She wants to create dances that show different kinds of endangered species."

"No way!" I said.

"Waaaay," Sarah replied. "She said there was the ocelot, which is a small, like, bobcat, and there's the Karner blue butterfly, which is bright blue, and something called the swamp panther, which is black and lives in the Florida Everglades. She's always trying to come up with ideas that let the kids in my sister's dance class use their imaginations, since they're all around six or seven years old. They'll have a performance in four weeks, whenever that is."

"That sounds beautiful."

"Totally beautiful. She makes the kids go home and get stuff for costumes, but she's really into the environment, so she asks them not to buy anything new. Last year, they were comets and shooting stars, and she made them go home and save up all the tinfoil and pie plates they were going to put in the recycling bins, and, I swear, the whole theater smelled like fried chicken." She checked her watch and said, "Lydia's going to be here in about ten minutes. You want to walk up the street and stare at that Kyle guy again?"

I tried to sound very calm and casual as I told her, "Okay, but he's going to be my boyfriend. I'll find you another one, if you'd like."

Sarah didn't look horrified, which was a huge relief, since I thought I sounded more ridiculous than I'd expected. "Oh, please," she said, laughing, as she stood up and wiped her hands on her shorts. "He's too old for either of us."

"I know," I lied. "Actually, can you come in and help me pack up my camera?"

"Oh, yeah, sure," she said, proving that she wasn't as obsessed with Kyle as I was. I looked down the street. His truck wasn't there, anyway.

"Do you have any ideas about who could be the other frogs?" I asked.

"I almost forgot to tell you!" she said, happy that I'd reminded her. "How about Curt Harrison? He's hilarious." I agreed. "He could be Medicine Frog," she went on.

"Would he treat this like a joke?" I asked, remembering his fake opera in English class.

"No, I'm sure he wouldn't. He's a good guy."

We looked at the phone and phone book next to it.

Sarah was the first to move. "It'll take two minutes," she said, scanning the phone book for his name. I noticed her long thin fingers and felt another completely annoying pang of jealousy.

We can be two *girls with poise and beauty*, I thought to myself. *Two girls, not just one.* Look at how she was helping me! She believed in me! She hooked her great hair over her ear as she dialed. *Two girls can be pretty, can have their own style.* If I couldn't beat this jealousy, I'd have to use some of my money for an appointment on the therapist's couch with Joyce. I was sure she'd be thrilled.

Curt was home.

"Hiya," Sarah said a little nervously, "this is Sarah Smythe. . . . Hi. Would you like to be in a movie? Amalee Everly's making it. You'd play a frog. . . . No, it's not a horror film." She smirked at the phone. "It's like a documentary, but fun. It should be fun. We really want you to do it. We think you'd be great. You'd just come in and do your part, in, like, three weeks. Right, Amalee?" I nodded.

There was a long pause as Curt considered. Sarah added something: "I think you should have been cast as Tevye in the play, just so you know. I liked working with Jordan, but your audition was hilarious."

Sarah got off the phone as Lydia pulled up. "He'll do it!" Sarah said excitedly. "This is going to be awesome!"

We jumped in the car and sped off to dance school in time to catch the end of her sister Julie's class.

Ms. Farraday, wearing tangerine tights, a tangerine leotard, and a black dance skirt, a tall pile of black hair balanced on her head, winked at us when we came in.

"Children," she said in a light Irish accent, "let's take the last ten minutes to try something new. What animal would you like to be?"

One boy immediately said, "Monkey!" and all the other kids agreed.

"Lovely," Ms. Farraday said. "All right, we are in the jungle, and you are very young monkeys practicing your jumping skills. You know that soon you'll be called upon to climb the trees and pick the bananas, so you want to show your families that you will be ready for the task." She didn't even say "Go!" but the little dancers were already in flight, screeching and somersaulting and, of course, jumping straight up in the air.

In a few minutes, Ms. Farraday said, "There will be no shortage of bananas this year, not with this group of jumpers! But now, *shhhh*, it is starting to rain, and you must find shelter under the low-lying broad banana leaves, huddling against one another, trying to stay warm and dry. And remember, you are not *like* monkeys. You *are* monkeys."

Sarah, Lydia, and I all widened our eyes. The jumping and screeching had been very monkeylike, but it was amazing to see these little kids really become monkeys, creeping under invisible leaves, shaking raindrops off their fur, gazing up from under leaves to look for a sign of the sun, and crouching against one another.

Ms. Farraday told them to, as monkeys, gather their things to go home. Then she turned to us.

"Children are inspired by nature," she said, as if to explain why the dancers were so hypnotizing. "I will bring in some videos of endangered animals and point out the movements that make these animals unique. I think I will also tell them that these animals could become extinct. Children have a remarkable sympathy for other living creatures. I don't want to scare them, but I think this will encourage performances that honor these animals."

"I would love to film the performance," I said.

"I'm so glad. I think there's nothing so persuasive as poetry to spur us into saving the environment. In this case it's the poetry of movement."

"This is incredibly nice of you," I said. "And you," I added, turning to Sarah.

"Yes," Ms. Farraday said to Sarah, "thank you for letting me know about this project. I'm new in the area. It will be fun to be involved with something."

"Did you come here from Ireland?" Lydia asked.

"Oh, no — I just got married, and we moved up here from Brooklyn, hopefully to raise some nice Irish-Jewish children."

Lydia let Julie continue to be a monkey in the car as long as she wore her seat belt. We stopped for ice cream, and Julie got a banana split.

"I guess you're not such an evil stepmother after all," Sarah said as we ate our ice cream. I thought Lydia was great, mother or stepmother. She laughed, so this must have been an ongoing joke.

She turned to me and said, "I found my calling as a stepmother."

"And my mother is very grateful," Sarah added. I knew Sarah's mother lived and worked in New York City, and that Sarah would go to visit her sometimes. Lydia worked at a natural food store called Green Pastures.

"Of course, I couldn't be a stepmother to just anyone," Lydia said. Was this really what Sarah wanted? She seemed happy with the arrangement. I felt sad that I didn't have a mother off to the side, just to have lunch in the city every once in a while, just to check in. I could have been happy with that, too. But I didn't have that, and I reminded myself that what I had was fine.

Fine? My dad had to pay Joyce a dollar every time he used that word. How did I *really* feel? Joyce would ask me that. I felt sad, but I knew I shouldn't want something I couldn't have.

Lydia was talking to me. She was telling me the dates for Julie's dance concert. I started nodding as if I'd heard every word.

✿ CHAPTER TEN ✿

Boy Trouble and Biodiversity

When we got home, I went online and found the phone number for the Museum of Natural History in New York City. I called and, after punching a lot of numbers, was connected to the Hall of Biodiversity.

"Hallofbiodiversity," a busy-sounding voice said.

"Hi," I said weakly. "I'm making a film about endangered species, and I was wondering if I could talk to someone about food chains."

"Food chains? What kind of food chains?"

I followed Joyce's advice: *Relax and speak*. "The idea of food chains," I said.

The woman's voice sounded like it was getting irritated. "What do you mean? Have you been to our Web site? There's plenty of information there."

I tried one of Phyllis's tricks, even though I wanted to hang up. "Is there a supervisor I can speak with?"

No luck. "He's not here. And there's nothing he can help you with if all you can say is that you want to talk about food chains." So this was the person Ellen would be when she grew up. Her voice could wilt a head of lettuce.

"Okay, thank you," I said, hating that I was thanking her for nothing. I tried one more time. "So there's no one I could speak with if I came in?"

The voice sighed and said quickly, "Just a minute." Off the phone, she asked someone, "Is Gail here today?"

The other voice asked, "Which one?"

The woman I was talking to said, "She's researching the reserve for biodiversity."

And the other voice said, "No, but she's here all tomorrow."

Back on the phone, the woman said to me, "There's no one here." *Whatever you say, Ellen.* We both hung up.

I went to a corner of the big sheet of paper that said *The Web of Life/Food Chains* and wrote *Gail* and a smiley face.

Phyllis had said that if I wanted to go to New York, she'd come with me. I called her and asked if she could go tomorrow.

"It's pretty late notice," she said, "but, yeah, sure. We have to be home by five thirty so I can run the numbers at John's. And it's chicken potpie night. That's really why I want to get home."

I said I took that very seriously, and she thanked me.

That night I biked past Kyle's house — his truck wasn't there — and over to the tai chi people. As Kevin, the curly-haired man, had told me, they went through the poses of five animals: the crane, the tiger, the bear, the serpent, and the monkey. I filmed a few minutes of every pose.

After they were done, Kevin came over again and explained how each pose allowed them to feel the energy of different animals, and that each energy helped them to feel balance in their own lives.

"If I have to help a friend move and I have to lift a lot of boxes, I think of the bear with its enormous strength, how he anchors his legs and yet also moves with ease and playfulness. That helps me move gracefully as I carry the burden to help my friend."

I peeked from behind the camera. "Cool," I said.

Kevin smiled. "I was also thinking about endangered species. I like that you are including tai chi in your movie. We don't just need animals so that we can eat them or tame them or whatever we do to use them. We need them to inspire us, right? I was thinking about how we just need their energy. We need tigers and bears and cranes, and yet they are all endangered."

"What?" I asked. Had I heard him correctly?

"Well, not every one, but certain species. Like panda bears. We're breeding them in captivity just to keep them in the world. And do you know how many tigers there are left in the whole world? About seven thousand. There are over six billion people in the world and only seven thousand tigers. We breed them in captivity, too, just to help them survive. And in a country near India called Bhutan, the black-necked crane has a sacred history to the Bhutanese people and is important in their literature. They're endangered. You can't put your finger on why they're so important, but if you lost them, you'd lose a piece of history and a feeling of being close to God."

I loved how this camera made people talk. Adults had never spoken to me like this before.

Kevin invited me to do tai chi with his group any morning or evening, explaining that some people thought it could only be done in the morning, but his group loved the light and the feeling at the end of the day. Plus, he added, it meant they didn't have to get up at the crack of dawn. I told him I'd try.

On my way home, I looked over, as always, at Kyle's house. It was getting dark and shadowy, but I thought I saw someone on the doorstep. Kyle. But it wasn't just Kyle. As my bike swung past, I could see that it was Kyle making out with a brown-haired girl with long legs who was almost as tall as he was. I was able to stay silent as I rode, and I didn't fall off the bicycle, either. But I kept riding and riding, past my house and into the dark. I couldn't go fast enough.

This was against all the rules. I was never allowed to go out at night without wearing the orange reflective stripes that Phyllis had bought for me. But I kept going. I knew there was a long hill coming up. As I went over, I lifted my legs off the pedals and felt myself going almost as fast as I wanted.

At the bottom of the hill the road swerved off to the left. That's why I didn't see the car coming. It sped around the corner and up the hill when I was almost at the bottom. I jerked the handlebars just in time to turn away, but my front wheel hit something, a log or a rock, and I flew off the bike and bashed my shoulder into the fence in front of someone's house. The car kept on going, and I took a minute in the silence to make sure I was still alive.

I swung my arm. I stood up. I walked my bicycle up

the hill, just relieved that I could do it. If I had been three feet farther down the hill, I probably wouldn't be alive. I felt absolutely sure about one thing: I knew that this was how my mother had died. She wasn't like Betsy, jumping into a tree trunk canoe down the Amazon. She didn't lose control on purpose like Betsy did. She was out of control. I felt it in my blood, my mother's blood pounding in my heart as I walked up the hill, panting and shaking.

My dad and Phyllis were both at the house, standing at the end of the driveway.

"Where were you?" Dad called out.

"Where were you?" Phyllis repeated.

I looked down at Kyle's house out of habit. Could he see them yelling for me? The lights in his house were out at nine o'clock, and his car was in the garage. So he was in the dark with that girl.

Phyllis was still holding her doggie bag from dinner at John's restaurant. "Where are your reflective stripes? What were you doing out after dark without your stripes?"

I lied quickly and completely. "I'm so sorry. It was darker than I thought. Then my bike flipped on a stick that I didn't see, and I fell, and I walked for a while. Sorry."

Phyllis and Dad changed from questions to comfort.

"Where?" Phyllis asked. "Are you all right? Should we call Dr. Nurstrom?"

"I'm *fine*." That was a lie, too.

Dad took my bike to the garage and told me dinner was waiting inside. Phyllis walked me in. Was my wild mother such a good liar, too? If you were going to spend a lot of time out of control, you'd have to be good at lying to cover your tracks. I could already feel the ability to cover my bumpy, dangerous tracks.

But why? Because Phyllis and Dad would kill me if they knew what had happened. And I was embarrassed, too.

But then I realized they wouldn't kill me. In sixth grade, I had pushed a not-so-good friend, Lenore Nielson, down the stairs, because she told me my father, who was sick, was "dying." I didn't mean to hurt her or even to push her, let alone push her down the stairs, but that's what happened, and it was a horrific event. It felt like the whole school rose up against me. My dad's friends had been sympathetic, understanding, and helpful. They stuck up for me more than I felt I deserved.

But this was different. I really was out of control this time. I didn't want to tell Phyllis and Dad how upset I was, or why, but they didn't deserve to live with a person who lied all the time when all they ever did was let me know I could tell them the truth.

There was no good way to bring the truth up. We were already sitting down to dinner. The subject had been changed to my dad wondering where his own reflective stripes were. I decided to ask a few questions about my mother.

"That was really scary, flying through the dark like that. It actually made me think of Sally's accident." I was now even more careful not to call her my mother. "Didn't her car hit a tree? That must have been awful."

I looked up from my spinach lasagna. Phyllis and Dad looked up from theirs, too, and Phyllis had an *I told you this would come up someday* look on her face.

"She hit a tree," Dad said. Phyllis stared harder. "Unfortunately, there had been a few accidents there. It was a bad curve."

"Yes, it was a dangerous curve," Phyllis echoed, but with a funny look on her face. "Especially when . . . it was so dark."

Dad said, "Oh, yes, it was very dark. It was after midnight. They say that one of her headlights was out."

"Among other things," Phyllis said.

"It's so scary that it could have happened to anyone," I said. "You just never know." I could tell that there was something they weren't saying. The fact that my mother was "crazy" and "a child" had nothing to do with it?

"I guess so," Dad mumbled, quickly taking his plate to the kitchen.

He returned with ice cream. "You know what?" he said to Phyllis. "You tell her. It's fine with me, but I'd rather you told her. I'll just try to sugarcoat it, and I know you won't."

Phyllis seemed to relax. "True enough," she said. She turned to me. "The night of your mother's . . . accident, she shouldn't have been driving, and she knew it."

Phyllis folded her hands and looked at my dad, speaking as much to him as to me. "You see, Amalee . . . she was really, really drunk."

CHAPTER ELEVEN

Animals Are Everywhere

I couldn't sleep that night. Phyllis and Dad's voices murmured at the kitchen table until at least eleven o'clock, while I lay in bed and felt the wild blood pumping in my body. I remembered how angry I'd felt when I'd pushed Lenore in sixth grade. And then I remembered how upset I'd been as I sped downhill on my bike. I couldn't imagine my dad doing any of these things. That was my mom in me. What would happen when *I* drank alcohol? Would I be able to stop? Would I feel wilder? And who could answer questions about how much of this stuff you can actually inherit from a parent? Phyllis made it all clear: Now I understood my dad's sadness when he talked about Sally, everyone's uncomfortableness when they tried to come up with words to describe her, and, I realized, how much everyone avoided talking about her. What had

Joyce said? That Sally was always late for work, and that Dad was always covering up for her. It all made sense now. But this was about me, too. If Sally, my own mother, was so out of control all the time, was I a ticking time bomb counting down to crazy?

I woke up in the morning without knowing I'd fallen asleep. I told myself to get it together. *You don't know who you are or who you will become, but that doesn't have to be a bad thing.* I breathed evenly and got ready to go to New York City. I remembered the light that had been so beautiful on the tai chi people. *Plug the camera into the TV set and see if it came out as well as you'd hoped*, I told myself. *Stock up your camera bag and think of questions for Gail, if we find her.* Then, as if I was doing tai chi, I tried to act like a bear, steadily plodding along into the living room, slow and easy, pulling out the cables to plug into the camera. Out of habit I looked out and saw Kyle's truck in his driveway. I felt sick. I didn't want to look at the film or do anything productive, and I didn't want breakfast. I didn't feel like a strong bear — more like a flock of cranes flying in all directions. Is this when my mother would start to drink?

"Plug in the camera," I commanded myself softly, and I put the cable in and turned on the TV. Beautiful! The sun was so bright at some angles that it looked like it had carved the tai chi people into little stick figures. But then there was more footage, later, where I was close enough to capture the looks of peaceful concentration on their golden faces.

Maybe everyone had to make the effort to slow way down or else they'd go flying over their own handlebars. Maybe that's why the tai chi people did tai chi.

"Kyle has a skinny, tall, beautiful girlfriend, but *two* people can be beautiful, and everyone has their own style," I told myself, out loud since Dad had already left for work.

Phyllis arrived fifteen minutes later and we drove to the train station. She was silent for almost two minutes, which was a first for her.

"So, are you angry with me?" she asked.

"Of course not," I said. In fact, I was amazed Phyllis had been able to keep the secret about my mother for so long.

"Your dad is not happy with me," she said. "After you went to bed, he said he wished we'd waited a few years to tell you about your mom."

"He's wrong." I said. "You were right."

"I was thinking about it. I didn't break it to you gently."

"I'm not angry," I repeated. How she told me was not

the problem. "So, does this mean my mother was an alcoholic?"

"Yes," she said. "With some people it's a fine line. They just drink a lot. But the definition of alcoholism is that alcohol interferes with your work or your personal life, and alcohol interfered with everything your mother did. That's just a fact. Even your dad knew it eventually."

"Was she born an alcoholic?" I asked.

"Maybe. Nobody knows if you're born with it or whether or not you inherit it." She looked at me.

"So I could have it," I said.

"Maybe, but I don't think so," Phyllis said.

"Why not? How do you know?" I asked. I wasn't angry. I hoped I didn't sound angry.

"You don't remind me of your mother," Phyllis explained. "You remind me of . . . well, you remind me a little of me." She was silent for another record two minutes.

When we got to the train station, I insisted on buying our tickets. "Okay," she said, "but I'm getting lunch. I want to go to a nice restaurant."

"I'm not hungry," I said as we got on the train, but not loud enough for her to hear.

I felt a little relieved that Phyllis, the practical planner, thought I was like her. She seemed embarrassed by what she'd said, however, so I let her change the subject and keep it changed.

I told her that I was getting information, but I still didn't have anything for Frog X, the not-useful species that we protect for the sake of protecting it.

"Hm, I can understand your problem there. Maybe you should talk to your dad. If the reasons you save Frog X are not practical, they're philosophical. He's a philosopher."

"Practically stated," I said, and thought about how practical Phyllis was, and again how she thought that I was like her. That made me stand a little taller and straighten the strap on my camera bag.

We were now in Grand Central Station, admiring the constellations painted on the ceiling. *Animals are everywhere*, I thought, *even in the sky*. Phyllis scanned the subway map and got us on the shuttle heading west, then on the C train to get to the museum.

Usually when I was in the city, I looked at things like noses or hairstyles or eyes, but today all I saw was animals and plants. Buttons were shaped like flowers; one woman had a toucan bird-shaped clasp on her purse; there were barrettes with elephants on them; there was a tote bag with a misty photo of a rain forest; and every school shirt had a mascot, like a tiger or a ram.

Somehow I felt Frog X here, but I couldn't tell why. Protecting it was important, and I felt like the reason was right here with us in this subway car. We reached the Museum of Natural History stop, with its tile mosaics of grand animals superimposed on their extinct ancestors and bronze imprints of their footprints. I thought about how on the subway, people kept their plants and animals almost hidden, as if they were saying, "I have an animal on my shirt, but don't worry, I'm reading this paper. I'm a human who thinks about humans, and buildings, and money. Human things." But here at the museum stop, all the animals were right out in the open, stamping around the walls, fur and teeth and tails, and people were flooding out of the subway cars with us to spend the day with them.

"I'm so glad we're here!" Phyllis said, echoing my excitement. Then she added, "I'm not going to say a word during the interview." She took me by the shoulders and putting me squarely in front of her as we entered the museum. We went up the stairs. After looking at the long line, Phyllis decided to become a museum member so we could wing our way through the short line. That was nice of her.

Soon we found the Hall of Biodiversity, glowing darkly like a forest with the sun barely shining through the branches. The forest turned out to be a copy of a nature reserve in the middle of the Central African Republic, and there were descriptions of all the things that were threatening the huge area of forest.

Next to the replica of the forest, there were flat television panels with an ongoing stream of information flashing across them. Underneath was information written on clear plastic panels, and Phyllis pointed out that each of those panels related to a part of the planet that was particularly fragile, like islands, forests, and coral reefs. All the information was pointing to how quickly these places were disappearing.

Across the way, there was a huge wall with fake (or so I hoped) animals pinned up in huge fountains of small to large animals, like fountains of life.

"Are those food chains?" I asked Phyllis.

"No, I think it shows animals that are related to each other," Phyllis observed.

There were sea turtles and frogs and insects of every color and strange shape, starting with things like beetles at the bottom and getting bigger and bigger. "Maybe they're just trying to show the everythingness of everything," I said, and Phyllis laughed.

"Yeah, I was just thinking maybe all they're doing is showing us how cool the world is by just lighting it well.

I'm not sure how they're all connected," she said. "Hey, here's a food chain."

There was a clear panel running like a long counter below the animals on the wall. Phyllis and I read about sea otters. Sea otters eat sea urchins. Sea urchins eat kelp. A huge number of sea creatures, including fish, of course, live in the kelp, and seabirds eat the fish. If there aren't enough sea otters — and at one point they were more endangered than they are now — there are too many sea urchins, and they eat all the kelp, so the sea creatures who lived in the kelp have no place to live. Then the birds don't have anything to eat. I started writing all this down.

We also saw an example of an animal that warns us, like the mutated frogs, that we could be in danger ourselves. Mussels, which look like clams, filter water all the time, but since they filter about a gallon of water every two hours, they're easily hurt by water pollution. When mussel populations go down, scientists get worried.

We walked around for another ten minutes before I felt overwhelmed.

"This shows the webs of life, shows their beauty, shows the warnings we get from the environment. . . . What do I have to add to this?" I was glad I'd said it out loud.

"Well, why do you think you should make a film about this?" Phyllis asked.

"That's just it — I'm not sure I should!" I yelled in a whisper.

"Argh, I'm such a bad therapist." Phyllis sighed. "I was trying to get you to say for yourself what I want to say, which is that you, Amalee Everly, bright, unusual young woman that you are, will put your stamp on your film. You will make your film. Look at all of this stuff that is disappearing! They shouldn't call this the Hall of Biodiversity — they should call it the Hall of Boy Are We in Trouble. We need many different voices to speak for the many different species, right?"

"Thank you, Phyllis," I said, turning away to read a panel about the dangers of clear-cutting forests. I felt embarrassed by such a big compliment, but also back on track.

"I can see why this is too much, though," she agreed. "Let's talk to this Gail person if we can find her. Or let's let you talk to her."

I went to the information desk and asked for Gail.

"Gail who?" the volunteer asked a little suspiciously.

"She's doing work on a reserve for the Hall of Biodiversity," I explained.

"But what's her *name*?" the woman interrupted.

Phyllis surprised me, the way she sometimes did, with a little lie. "She said her name so fast, we don't know what it is. I should have asked her to spell it. She said there were two of them here!" She laughed apologetically.

"So she's expecting you?" the woman asked.

"We're early," I said.

"She's still at lunch," the woman said. Then, out of the blue, she added, "You know, she goes to that fancy coffee place where she can plug in her computer and do the Internet."

"Oh, the one on Columbus?" Phyllis asked. "That's funny, I thought that was her in the window."

"Yeah, that was her," the woman said.

Phyllis and I made a plan. First we had to tell each other what good liars we were. Then we agreed that we would find this woman and tell her what I was up to and ask if we could meet her back at the museum.

In the café, we found a woman with long brown hair held back with two clips that had giraffes on them. She was the only woman there with a laptop computer. We stood and stared at her for a moment. She looked up nervously from her computer screen.

"May I help you?" she asked politely.

"Yes," I said, pleased that my voice sounded clear. "Are you Gail?"

"Yes," she answered.

I dived in. "I'm making a film about endangered species, and I was wondering if I could talk to you about food chains or, um, the web of life. The people at the museum said you were the person to talk to."

The woman looked panicked. She bit her lip and then said, a bit impatiently, "You can go to the museum Web site and got lots of information. Have you done that?"

"Yes, it's just that I wanted to talk with a person," I croaked. Phyllis cleared her throat. I was caught between two nervous women. One didn't want to talk to me, and one wanted me to ask the other one to talk.

"I guess I was wondering if there was . . ." *Relax and speak, relax and speak.* "I want to show that one reason to protect species is that they all fit in a food chain, and I was wondering if you could recommend a food chain that you think is interesting." How stupid did that sound? Ellen and Hallie popped into my head to say it sounded plenty stupid. But then Sarah popped in and said that Ellen and Hallie were stupid, and Phyllis cleared her throat again.

"Is this something you know about?" I asked.

"Yes," the woman said cautiously.

"I've heard that you're really interested in this stuff."

"I am. It's just that . . ." she said, and suddenly, like

Ms. Hazlett at the bank, she relaxed her shoulders, looked at Phyllis, and said, "What's that word that means dread, when you have a sense of . . . a sense of — agh! What is that word?"

"Foreboding," Phyllis said without a pause.

"That's it!" Gail exclaimed happily. "I'm writing a letter to my future mother-in-law about the caterer she wanted me to use for my wedding. I didn't want to say I dreaded using him." She typed as she spoke. "I'll just say I have a sense of foreboding about how busy he is. There. That won't offend her, will it?"

"Not at all. In fact, you're implying that she's chosen a caterer who is in demand and therefore a good choice," Phyllis pointed out.

"Phew!" Gail said, typing a few more words and pressing the SEND key.

"It's hard to disagree with your future mother-in-law," Phyllis sympathized.

"It sure is. She's an Upper East Side society lady, too. Champagne tastes and easily offended," Gail blurted out.

Phyllis nodded. I had no idea what was being said, and I suspected Phyllis didn't, either, but suddenly we both loved this quirky woman in an old cotton sweater with no makeup and a future mother-in-law who liked champagne.

Gail clapped her hands and said, "That was a relief. Okay, you got me. I want to help you. I'm not sure that I can, but let's see. Can you come back to my office?"

Five minutes later, she'd waved us through the museum and into her office, which was filled with souvenirs from many adventures. There were pictures of friends next to each of them. There was a piece of stone that was cut into a thin slice that looked like the view of a tropical sea from an airplane. It must have had seventeen shades of green and blue. It was labeled AUSTRALIAN TURQUOISE. Next to it was a photograph of a smiling friend with a loose, messy ponytail standing next to a kangaroo. There was also a long feather labeled AMERICAN EAGLE next to a picture of a man standing with a majestic snowcapped mountain behind him. There was a bright red choker of beads hanging over a picture of a friend from Africa. Under the picture was a small label that just said, NAOMI, UGANDA 1999.

Gail started to open some files on her computer. Then she turned to me and said, "Let's go to Asia, shall we? That's where I've spent the most time. India, to be exact."

She took us to a Web site that was all about the Western Ghats of India.

"This is a Web site about a coastal region in western India. It's a hodgepodge of different terrains, including rain forest and plains. What's amazing is that you can't get to some of the densest forest, because it grows up so much during the rainy season. You know what I wish we could do? I wish we could get those little spaceships that they sent to Mars but drop them down with night-vision cameras into the middle of this forest. I would spend the rest of my life documenting the wildest of wildlife."

"Why don't you do that?" I asked.

"Hoo boy, where do I start? With money, I guess. It starts and ends with money. Come to think of it, it probably wouldn't work. There are fewer tree branches to get stuck in on Mars."

Gail pulled up some images of animals. There were jackals, elephants, leopards, panthers, crocodiles, tigers, and some animals I'd never heard of, like the Nilgiri langur, which was a monkey, and Nilgiri tahr, which looked like a mountain goat.

"What's that?" I asked, pointing to a little creature whose head was mostly eyes, under which was a tiny pointed nose and nervous little mouth.

"That's a slender loris," Gail said proudly. "They are awesome. They come out at night. It's very rare to see one."

"Are they a good example for a food chain? If you took

them away, would a whole lot of other animals I've never seen before disappear?"

"Depending on your definitions, everything you see here is endangered, from the loris to the leopard, but it's overall habitat threatened by human development and climate change, not one thing that's taken away, leaving the whole food chain in jeopardy. Oh, dear, I guess this isn't exactly what you asked for. There are animals that are listed as endangered. . . ." Gail said.

I still knew I could use this. "Can I get pictures of the ones on the endangered list?" I asked. "In fact, if I made a list, does this museum have pictures of a lot of different species that I could show in my movie?"

"Sure. I could arrange that. Meanwhile, why don't I tell you the basics of a food chain. Would that help? They show it close to the Dzanga-Sangha rain forest display in the Hall of Biodiversity. Here's the deal —"

"Would you mind if I filmed you while we did this?" I asked.

"Oh!" she gasped. "Just a minute." She left, then reappeared as Phyllis and I were reading an article about a tiger reserve and looking at pictures. Gail had brushed her hair, and was wearing mascara and lipstick.

"Let's get out of this office and find a prettier place."

We found a big display case that showed a grassy desert. She called it a savannah, or a wide grassy field, and said there were places like that in the Western Ghats. To tell the truth, what I liked was that it just went really well with Gail's sweater. The light was perfect, too.

"Food chains can be very basic," she began. "Nutrients in the soil feed the plants, and animals eat the plants. Those animals are herbivores, plant eaters. They do two important things. First, they poop, and second, they eventually die. Both functions put nutrients back in the soil. Or these animals are eaten by other animals who poop and die. Either way, these animals are putting nutrients back in the soil that feeds the plants. And then the plants feed the animals, and the cycle is complete. Now, some food chains go way beyond the basics. There are areas that teem with life, which allows for an incredible diversity of species, meaning very specific plants are eaten by very specific animals, so if one very specific plant or animal disappears, a whole, unique chain disappears. If that chain is somehow connected to another chain — and most of them are — that second chain gets out of whack, too. And so on, and so on.

"Plus," she continued, "if you take away the specific habitat of a plant or animal, you also destroy a delicate balance. You can break the chain by removing the place where the chain exists."

I spoke up. "Like if there are too many sea urchins and they eat all the sea kelp, then all the things that live in the kelp have no place to live."

"Someone has been to the Hall of Biodiversity at the American Museum of Natural History!" Gail said approvingly. "But also, if you turned parts of the Nilgiri Reserve, say the rain forest, into farmland, you may compromise a habitat beyond recovery and lose a beautiful little pocket of unique flora and fauna."

"Is that what you study?" I asked. "Do you study the beautiful little pockets?"

"Yes, that's what I do. Every day. It's an infinite pursuit, and I love it." And without waiting for another question, Gail looked right into the camera and said, "I think my favorite part of all this is that we can get deeper and deeper into understanding the way things are, but we'll never have a perfect understanding. There is so much complex diversity. We'll never perfectly replicate the intricacy of interrelationships that actually exist in a natural system. And yet every level of understanding we reach is really wonderful in and of itself. It's like we keep on painting a picture of what we see, but it's not the thing itself. Nature is a wonderful, exciting, endless mystery."

I looked down at my questions and didn't like them anymore.

I started winging it, as Phyllis would say. "Why don't you just tell us the name of the area you're studying in India and repeat some of the information you told us in your office."

Gail did this, explaining that her area of expertise was the Nilgiri Reserve in India and all the different parks and sanctuaries within it. She spoke with a straightforward friendliness that looked great on film. On a whim I asked her to imitate the slender loris, as she had unconsciously done when she'd described it to us in her office. She imitated it peering around in the dark.

When we were done and Gail was signing her permission paper, she asked, "Will you show this film someplace where I could see it?"

"I'll let you know. I hope so. But even if it's just at my house, we'll invite you over," I said.

As Phyllis and I walked out, Phyllis said, "I am amazed at how much she looked like a slender loris when she imitated it!"

We both laughed with joy and relief. We'd gotten what we wanted and then some. Now my heart was beating with excitement. I didn't feel out of control. I didn't want to be biking away from my life. I wanted to be here with Phyllis and all the footage of Gail in my camera.

"I don't think I'm out of control," I said as we walked to the restaurant.

"It's not a crime if you are, every now and then," Phyllis replied.

"Really?" I asked. Phyllis nodded. Still, I couldn't tell her about Kyle and what had happened last night. Instead, I went back to Lenore. "You know," I said, "I really did push Lenore by mistake last year. But wouldn't you say that a person who does something like that is . . . out of control?"

"If that's the definition of out of control, then everybody has a problem. We all do things in the heat of the moment, especially when we're young."

We walked in silence. For lunch, we went to a beautiful Japanese restaurant. We sat at a table next to a screen painted with a graceful flock of cranes. The waitress said I could film them. "They're good luck," she pointed out. Good luck to some, energy to the tai chi people, beautiful to me.

I wondered: If there were no such thing as cranes, would we miss them in some deep part of ourselves that we didn't know about?

Phyllis and I both ordered big bowls of noodles. "You know how I said you remind me of myself a little?" she asked. "Well, if I were you, I'd probably have a crush on that boy Kyle who lives down the street from you."

I forced my mouthful of noodles down and murmured, "He's got a girlfriend."

"He does? How do you know?"

"He lives down the street, remember? I saw them kissing in front of his house last night." I thought of all the times I'd looked over at his house and then remembered what a smart bunch of people Dad's friends were. Obviously, they'd seen me watching.

"Hm. When did you find that out? Before or after you fell off your bike?" Phyllis asked, not making eye contact.

"Before," I confessed quietly.

"So you wiped out after you saw them kissing?" Phyllis guessed.

"I wiped out because I was going too fast," I almost whispered.

"And you went fast because you saw them kissing?" Phyllis guessed again, this time correctly.

"Maybe," I said.

"And now you're wondering if you're out of control somehow, especially after learning what you've learned about your mother." I didn't say anything, so she went on. "Well, speaking for myself, if I had a thing for Kyle and I saw him kissing someone, I might have peeled out on my bike, too. And I do not consider myself to be out of control. I don't think anyone would describe me that way."

We both laughed a little. I thought of her alphabetizing my dad's medicine cabinet after he was sick and giving him a pill case that marked the days of the week for all the medications he still had to take. She was definitely in control.

"How's your shoulder?" she asked, easing us off the topic.

Gratefully I said, "Better." I did feel much better, and not just in my shoulder.

We got home in the early evening, along with the tired commuters.

Dad was home, so we all sat and watched my new footage on the television. It would be a nice contrast with Henry at the aquarium as he stood next to the light rippling through the water. Where Gail stood, it was all very still, in a museum way.

"She's a kicker," Dad said.

"You can't tell until she starts talking about plants and animals," Phyllis said. "Amalee had to draw her out."

"Good for you," Dad murmured, still listening to Gail. "Wow, she really makes you care about this stuff."

I asked, "What do we do to preserve the web of life — in this house, I mean?"

Dad groaned, and Phyllis laughed. "Probably not enough," Dad said. "But I drive a fuel-efficient car, we recycle, we compost . . . uh." He looked nervous. "Oh, and we use recycled paper whenever we can, and I give money to environmental organizations, and, and . . . I don't water the lawn. I'm not a vegetarian, but thanks to John, most of our food comes from a local source."

Phyllis shook her head. "I'm not sure if that's enough, David."

Dad said, "I planted trees to shade the house in the summer so we don't have to use air conditioning as much, and we use energy-efficient appliances and lightbulbs."

Phyllis said, "I don't know. . . ."

"I try to salvage things instead of throwing them away," Dad went on.

"Stop torturing Dad!" I yelled, laughing with Phyllis.

"I should get a solar panel," Dad said to himself.

"You *should*," Phyllis teased him. "Oh, you forgot to mention growing native plants that attract birds and butterflies." She turned to me and said, "Your dad has *always* been into the environment."

“Was my . . . was Sally?” I asked. Phyllis and I had been through so much today, I felt like I could ask.

Dad smiled sadly. “That’s a good question. Yes, she would have been if she hadn’t had all those problems. She loved animals.”

“Yes,” Phyllis agreed, “she could have been very happy taking care of animals. In fact, I could see her in a place like southern Argentina, very far away from her mother, looking after seals and penguins.”

That night I dreamed that I was standing in the desert, and a woman who was Gail or Betsy or Phyllis or my mother was telling me to look again. I saw penguins on an ice shelf and saw that I was really on the South Pole. Then suddenly I was in a tropical jungle surrounded by huge trees with monkeys.

“Don’t think small,” the woman told me. “Everything is connected.”

✿ CHAPTER TWELVE ✿

The Mutant and the Merely Mean

I realized the next morning that I was ready to start writing the script for the movie. It started with John, who would be the head frog. He would say that, as a frog living on the banks of a pond, he was grateful that people were doing so much to protect both the land and the water, because if either the land or the water were polluted, he'd be in trouble. By protecting plants and animals, we were protecting ourselves, because we were all part of the web of life.

Then Curt would say that plants and animals give us medicine, food, clothes, and even ideas for everything from bandages to airplanes.

Next, Sarah would step forward and say that the things that endanger frogs can warn us about what may be endangering us. She would mention the mussels that I learned about at the museum and say that if their numbers declined, it could be a sign that the water was extremely polluted.

After that, Marin would come in and say that plants and animals are beautiful and inspiring to us.

Finally Frog X would step up and say . . . what? I wasn't sure about that part yet.

I read what I'd written. It all seemed so obvious. Despite myself, I looked out the window to see if Kyle's truck was in the driveway. It wasn't. I grabbed my camera and went down the street to the little bit of swamp to try to find the mugwort that Betsy had told me about. It should be in bloom. She said that people swore by mugwort's ability to make them dream more at night. I wasn't sure where I'd put this information, but I had to do something. Sarah was supposed to come over in a little while, and I'd ask her what she thought.

Not only did I catch the mugwort in bloom, it was also in a very nice little patch of sun. It had simple, white flowers, but they looked almost magical on camera. I admired all the other plants around it.

I saw Kyle's truck coming down the street as I emerged from the woods. I sped up and hoped I could pass his driveway before he parked. I wasn't going to make it. I looked over my shoulder and noticed that he wasn't alone. He was with his girlfriend!

"Hey, Amalee," he called out as I passed. "Hey, this is Amalee," he said to his girlfriend. "She's making a film about environmental science, right?"

"About endangered species," I corrected him, smiling and terrified. His girlfriend had long and very shiny hair, big red lips, and beautiful brown eyes. *Two girls can be pretty*, I thought . . . but it wasn't working.

"What do you mean?" she asked. Not meanly, but not nicely, either.

"I'm making a film about why it's important to preserve endangered species," I said.

"No *duh*," she said. "So why are you making a film? Hasn't it already been done?"

"I don't know," I answered, trying to be nice, and also being honest. Somehow being honest didn't seem like the right thing to be right now. I saw a shadow coming up behind me and I looked. It was Sarah. I didn't want her to see this, but it was too late.

"This is Erica," Kyle said, still pretending the conversation was going okay.

"This is Sarah," I said.

"Every time I'm flipping past the nature channel or

whatever it is on TV, they're talking about endangered species," Erica said to Kyle, as if I wasn't even there anymore.

"Amalee's film is more interesting than that. It's funnier," Sarah said. She was finding the words I wanted to say.

"Funny?" Erica couldn't seem to believe it. "A funny movie about endangered species? Ha-ha."

"Well, it does require some imagination and *intelligence* to picture it," Sarah said with a smile. "We should get back to work," she added, and we started to walk away. While we were still close enough for Erica and Kyle to hear, she said, "I can't wait to see your new footage from the Museum of Natural History."

I started to say I didn't know if I was ready to show it, but she shook her head and looked back. "I was just trying to sound serious," she explained quietly. Kyle and Erica were already in his house. "I take it back! You're not too young for him, and you should try to steal him away from Dumbo over there."

"She had a point," I said.

"No, she had no point. You can argue that *Fiddler on the Roof* has been done before, so why do it again? Why do anything? She's just jealous."

"Okay, that's really nice of you to say, but you can't make me believe that she's *jealous*!" I protested.

"She is!" Sarah cried. "She knows that Kyle likes you."

I remembered when Kyle had said, *Girls who like science are cool*. Had he said that to her?

"I started the script," I said to Sarah. "And it seems kind of dumb. . . ."

"Not as dumb as her," Sarah muttered, and we both chuckled as I pulled the script out.

Sarah mouthed some of the words as she read it. "This is good," she said. "It makes sense when I say it out loud."

"I just want to make it simple at first, but it seems too simple."

"No, not too simple. Think about it. When you're on a stage, there's so much to see and hear, especially at first. No, you did this right. You're going to have these five giant frogs introducing themselves. That's a lot for the audience to take in. It's going to be really theatrical. You don't want really complicated language to overwhelm them at first." I didn't care that she was acting like an expert. I was willing to believe she *was* one!

"Who do you think should play this Frog X?" she asked.

"I have no idea," I said.

"I do, but you might not like it. Did you know that Ellen Shapiro moved away?"

This was *the* Ellen.

"No way," I gasped. I couldn't believe that Ellen would be in my head even after she was actually gone.

"So, how about Hallie?" Sarah asked quietly.

"Hallie? No," I answered. I had told Sarah about how mean Ellen and Hallie had been, and how mean I had felt when I was around them.

"Her little sister is in my sister Julie's dance class. She's totally different now. I think she's a little scared."

"Scared of what?" I asked.

"She has no friends," Sarah said, and I immediately knew she was right. I hadn't had any other friends when I'd been friends with Ellen and Hallie, either. They were too snobby.

"She actually started talking with me at the dance class, and I told her what you were doing. She looked sad and said it sounded really great."

"She did?" Really??

"And I told her that Ms. Farraday was making a special set of dances for the movie. I guess I was rubbing it in at that point," Sarah admitted. "But then I felt bad, because as I was leaving, she said to let her know if she could help. Um, and I felt so bad that I said I knew you'd really like that. And she looked happy."

"No! No! No way! No!" I yelled. "You think she's nice, and then she gets you with something that is completely awful. I'd rather have *Lenore*." That wasn't true, I realized. Even though I felt bad that I'd pushed Lenore down the stairs, and I was glad she'd forgiven me, I didn't want to be Lenore's friend again. She couldn't help trying to make me feel bad. I realized that I believed Hallie could help it. She did know better. Especially when Ellen wasn't around.

"*Lenore* . . ." Sarah said. "It's funny you should mention Lenore. I saw her mom at the bank."

I looked at Sarah and projected a very specific message through my eyeballs: *You are not going to tell me to put Lenore in my movie.*

Sarah looked back at me with a message coming through her eyeballs: *Um . . . yes, I am.*

"Lenore wants to be involved, too. Her mom told me."

I dropped my head into my hands. I knew I could tell Sarah that she had no business bothering me with all this. But she wasn't insisting, and I noticed what she had done: She had made my movie sound interesting to Hallie so Hallie would regret being mean to me. Maybe she had done the same thing with Lenore's mom. She'd just done too good a job.

"C'mon, couldn't they help us with our costumes or something? Just come to one of my sister's dance classes. Hallie picks up her sister at class. We just missed her last time."

"Okay, I'll talk to her, and maybe — *maybe* — I can ask her to do something like hold a microphone. But she's not Frog X. Frog X is the most helpless. She should be the smallest, and she shouldn't have a — a history of being a bully."

"Who do we know who's little?" Sarah asked out loud.

"Your sister," I said, just as she was about to say it.

"My sister," she echoed, and we felt as if we'd just found the one and only answer.

I imagined Julie balancing the huge frog head on her shoulders. Carolyn would help make it lighter and attach something to make it fit comfortably.

"She'll totally do it. I'll make her," Sarah said.

I was still thinking of the little body with the big head. The smallest, the least helpful, the unimportant. I could feel an enormous sadness coming on. I said I had to go to the bathroom, and once I got there, I buried my head in a towel and just cried. I didn't know why. I splashed my face and thought about awful Lenore, which made me stop. I started thinking what kind of out-of-the-way job I could give *her*, like traffic patrol.

I came out of the bathroom to find Sarah holding a stack of envelopes. "Mail's here," she said.

I opened the envelope from the Minnesota Pollution Control Agency, the first people to send me the information I'd asked for. There were photos of the deformed frogs that had been discovered by the students. The letter said it was still a mystery what had caused the deformities, but one of their first theories was that they were from dioxins, which came from bleaching with chlorine. The letter also mentioned that amphibious populations were down throughout the Great Lakes region, meaning there were fewer and fewer frogs all over the American Midwest.

Sarah and I looked at the photos. A few frogs had an extra back leg, smaller and sticking out to the side. Some others had deformed legs, and one had only one eye. The other eye simply wasn't there. "What caused this?" Sarah murmured over my shoulder.

"They think maybe pollution from a chemical called dioxin."

"This is terrible. I'd say it's gross, but I feel so sorry for them. I don't want to hurt their feelings." Sarah put her hand on my back and said, “You’re so cool, Amalee. We’re going to speak for these poor little frogs. There aren’t any actual two-headed frogs, are there?”

I said I didn’t think so.

But there could be one in the future. I’m sure no one had predicted a five-legged frog in the past.

The next day was rainy and perfect for sitting in pajamas and watching all the footage I had shot. I sat down with the remote control in my hand and my big pad of paper in front of me.

Every person had his or her own particular look and place. I felt bad when I saw a little shadow on Betsy’s face that made her look like she had a bruised forehead, or shadows against a wall that looked like an extension of Gail’s hair. One camera angle made Henry at the aquarium look like he had a dark ostrich egg growing out of his head. “You’d better get that looked at,” I told the television screen.

Relax and write, I told myself. I had the whole day.

I was lucky that I’d had good light for everyone. Dad’s friend Phil Novick had warned me that I would probably lose a good chunk of my work to poor lighting or bad sound. I’d made sure everyone put the microphone right up to their mouth, and my headphones let me adjust their volume or tell them to speak up a little. And I'd bought that disk of silver fabric that Joyce had held up to Henry. The silver fabric had reflected light from the ceiling bulbs near the aquarium. Also, the camera was supposed to be able to handle dim light. So, minus the few seconds of bruises and dark eggs, things looked more or less movie-ready.

I decided to write down the parts of everyone's interviews I would take for each frog or category. The only problem was that I didn't want to. So first I ate two bowls of cereal and a peach. Then I made batter for cookies. I sat myself down while the cookies were in the oven, and said I would at least try to create these categories until the cookies were ready.

I was prepared for the most boring and hardest part of the project, but it was as simple as putting things in different baskets, like the beauty basket, the medicine basket, or the food-chain basket. There were a few moments when I thought a comment fit into more than one category, showing that a plant or animal was both helpful and beautiful, but I just made a question mark next to each of these parts and moved on. Unfortunately, my nose told me the cookies were ready, which meant they were on the crispier side.

I was done in a few hours, including cookie trips to

the kitchen (four of them), a trip to the mailbox (Kyle's truck wasn't there), and a few minutes figuring out how to film the deformed-frog pictures (I'd do it outside when the weather cleared up).

I hoped that cutting and pasting all of the movie would be less scary than I'd imagined, too.

In the afternoon, I went on a bike ride. It was still sprinkling, but I had to get out. There was plenty to think about. Did Kyle really like that girl just because she was pretty? I picked up speed on my bike, but this time I wasn't scared. It felt good to go fast. Maybe I had some crazy blood. Maybe that would be a problem. Or maybe it was okay.

I went to John's restaurant with Joyce that night. Joyce picked us both up on her way, letting herself in to see my progress.

"That big pad certainly looks full of notes!" Joyce complimented me. "How is it all going?"

"I think it's all going fine," I said truthfully. "There's just one problem. I don't have much for Frog X. I don't have anything, really."

"Well, what exactly is Frog X?"

"Frog X is the frog who we may not need to help us kill mosquitoes or make any miracle medicines, and Frog X isn't beautiful. Frog X is just out there."

Again, I thought of Julie with the giant frog mask, and I felt sad again.

"Joyce," I said with alarm, changing the subject, "if Hallie wanted to work on my movie, should I let her?"

"Isn't she the one who wasn't nice to you?" Joyce asked.

"Yes, but her friend left, and now she doesn't have any friends."

"Was she the meaner of the two?" Joyce asked.

"No. She definitely wasn't."

"Well, some friendships bring out the worst in a person, so maybe she's not so bad now," Joyce observed. "I'd say you could give her a chance, but not a big one. You want allies for this!"

Joyce clearly wanted to jump-start me into solving my problem. "I want to press you here: What is this Frog X?" she asked. "What do you think is the argument to save Frog X?"

"Every animal is unique," I blurted out. "Each is like a work of art."

"Good. Is that it?"

"No. But, but . . . I don't know."

"Try," Joyce insisted, driving past John's restaurant so we could keep talking.

I was afraid if I tried, I'd start to cry and Joyce would pull over and try to hug me.

I took many deep breaths and asked myself why. Why? Animals and plants were all unique. We needed them even if we didn't need them to survive. And how did we know . . .

"I know the other reason we need to pay attention to Frog X," I said. "How do we *know* something is unimportant? How do we *know* what plant or animal will help us survive? We should let plants and animals survive no matter what, but what if there's a snail whose shell is the model for the perfect building of the future? What if mugwort makes you dream, and what if just one person's way to survive is to dream more? What if there's some tiny bug that eats pollution or . . . or a plant that soaks up acid rain? And you know what else? What if Frog X is not beautiful to me, but it's beautiful to someone else who needs that beauty to survive? Everyone needs different things to survive. Just because something isn't helpful to me doesn't mean it isn't helpful to someone else. Right?"

"Wow," Joyce said, finally pulling into the restaurant parking lot. "No wonder you were having a hard time deciding what to say. We preserve a frog because it may be useful to us. But we also preserve a frog even if it isn't useful to us. And now you're saying we also need to preserve a frog because there's such an enormous range of what we need to survive and we shouldn't presume to know what we need, or will need, or what other people need. Correct?"

Yes. Why was it so sad that a small, plain frog could be the key to one person's survival? Suddenly I knew I had to call my English teacher, Mr. Chapelle, to see if I could use some of the footage of his son with the dolphins. The way his film had shown it, dolphins did something, whether it was the way they moved or some secret language they spoke, that worked like a medicine for some people. Maybe it wouldn't work for me, but it would work for Mr. Chapelle's son.

In the restaurant, John teased me and said he was going to make me frog leg stew. He also asked if he was going to have to wear tights. I said no to the stew and no to the tights. He made me something like macaroni and cheese, but with potatoes. He said I would love it, and I did.

✿ CHAPTER THIRTEEN ✿

The Stories Are Coming Together

Things went quickly in the next week. Mr. Chapelle said I could take any part of his film for mine. He was surprised when I asked at first, but when I told him that I was making a film because of his assignment, he seemed pretty excited for me. My dad asked why I needed footage of Mr. Chapelle's autistic son. I told him to trust me.

I filmed the pictures of the deformed frogs, only to find out, when Gail sent me tons of pictures over the computer, that I could edit computer photos right into the film. I was learning two huge things at once: One was about endangered species, and the other was about how many cool things I could do to make a movie, even though I had to concentrate hard to make all the little details fit together.

I found a room next to Sarah's sister's dance class

where they said I could film the narrator frogs. And every night, I worked on the script, reminding myself that it was easier than homework.

At the end of the week, I made my first trip with my dad to New York. I slept all the way in on the train while he read a mystery novel. I took a groggy look at the constellations on the ceiling of Grand Central Station when we arrived. "Hello, animals," I greeted.

We took the subway downtown. My dad's old student, Phil Novick, had reddish-blond hair and a wild, scraggly look that made him look like he spent more time awake at night than during the day, like a New York City slender loris.

After introducing us, Dad told us he was "going out to shop for a few things." That meant he was heading up to the Strand bookstore about ten blocks away. The Strand was crammed top to bottom with every kind of book, old and new, that could fit on its miles of shelves. For something very specific, you'd probably be up a creek trying to find what you wanted, but for a sense of the everythingness of everything — like we'd felt in the Hall of Biodiversity — it was a great place to be.

Phil and I worked quickly. We put everything up on his office computer and started cutting and pasting in the same way you'd cut and paste words on a computer, except we did it with pictures and sound. Phil looked like he'd been born doing it. I felt like I hadn't been born so lucky. I had a hard time making the sound and pictures go together, and my edits came up too quickly or too late. Phil told me I'd get used to it, calling it a "learning curve." He went out for a cup of coffee and told me to edit two pieces together all by myself. He talked me through it, then left me alone. It almost worked, didn't work, totally didn't work, looked as if the computer was about to crash, and then it worked! One image practically flowed into another. Since Phil still wasn't back, I tried another edit, and it worked, too! I enjoyed the challenge of it, making the pieces fit together the way he'd shown me. I was officially interested in film. In my mind, I was showing Kyle footage I'd taken in the Ecuadorian rain forest, pointing out the important features of this or that unique ecosystem. I laughed out loud at myself and went back to editing. Phil walked in and nodded at my progress.

When Dad appeared a few hours later, he had a bag of lunch for me and a bag of books for himself. "The Strand?" I asked.

Dad turned the bag so I could see it. It said THE STRAND.

Phil told Dad I was "a natural." I pretended to let the compliment bounce right off me, but it went right in.

On the train ride home, I drew a little calendar for myself. It was already June 28. I could start filming the frogs in the first weeks of July. I'd work around John's schedule.

Dad looked up from a book called *Tough Guys Don't Dance* and said, "I'm sorry about the way you found out that your mom had a drinking problem. And I feel uncomfortable about what you think of the fact that she'd been driving drunk when she died."

What? I was far away in movie land, wondering if John should wear green pants or green shorts (definitely pants, I decided). There were a lot of details to figure out.

I put down my notes. I had planned to ask Dad for more of the story at some point, but I'd also wanted to let him take his time, considering how sad he'd looked when Phyllis had finally told me the truth. Somebody had to bring it up sometime, however, and so it was Dad, and the time was now. I closed my calendar.

"It was totally fine the way she told me," I said. "It explained a lot."

"What do you mean?" he asked.

"Well, it explains why everyone always looked so uncomfortable when you'd say she was a little crazy. You were all wondering how and when you'd spill the beans to me, right?"

"Yeah," Dad confessed. "But no, it's more than that. Now that she's gone," he said, choosing his words carefully, "I don't want to make everything simple. I don't want you to think that every part of her personality came from the fact that she was an alcoholic."

I thought of the note at the bottom of the supermarket receipt with the words *flower, power, tower, sour, shower*. I saw a girl who liked to play with words and who probably roamed around her big house with no one to talk to. I saw a girl with long hair and a basketball, making her mom buy flowers at the store.

"I don't see her that way," I said.

"Good. Thank you. It's very rare for a twelve-year-old to know that people are very complicated." He still didn't know that I knew more about her than he thought I did.

"Do you think you'd be with Sally if you met her today?" I asked.

"Maybe not — not if she didn't get help. I've seen this kind of stuff with students. I can get a pretty good hit on which kids are having trouble with drugs. They write papers that kind of wander into space, they fall asleep in class, and then they only show up for tests. Their skin is clammy and their eyes are unfocused. Your mom never looked unhealthy, but there were plenty of indicators that she was an addict from the way she acted."

"She wasn't an addict. She was an alcoholic," I said.

"An alcoholic is someone who's addicted to alcohol," Dad explained.

Now I felt like Dad was giving up on Sally before he'd given her a chance.

"But don't addicts need our help?" I asked.

Dad looked at the ceiling and said, "Oh, Sally, Sally, why have you put me in this position?" Then he looked at me and said, "We did the best we could, Amalee. After a while, it's only when you *don't* help them when they can finally get help. Real help to stop."

"I'm sorry. I believe you." Suddenly I remembered that this was Sally, a person I never knew, a friend that we all felt sorry for, didn't dislike, but also didn't know. I changed the subject for both of us.

"I like editing," I said. "I mean, I'm sure it could get boring, but I like how I got a computer to do something I told it to do."

"Much easier than a person, or even a dog," Dad said, smiling. "Think of all the people who get to work with computers after they realize they can't deal with people."

"Phil seems like he can deal with people."

"Oh, yeah, he's great with computers, but he also loves people. He's a real ladies' man, from what I hear."

I wouldn't go that far. All that unbrushed, scruffy hair!

Dad looked like he wanted to say something else, but then went back to reading his book. I went back to my schedule.

Dad did look up then. "You can ask me about Sally anytime you want," he said finally. He didn't sound like he wanted to talk about it, but it was still nice of him to offer.

✿ CHAPTER FOURTEEN ✿

Wallflowers in Bloom

Later that night, John burst through the doors of the restaurant kitchen to find me.

"I have something for you!" he exclaimed, pulling out a pair of green flippers from behind his back. "I can get you four other pairs, too. They have them at my health club. I just joined — I'm sure you can tell." He turned to the side. He still had a big belly.

Carolyn was picking dead leaves off the plants and spraying some of them with water. I asked her to come over and give me advice about costumes.

"Keep it simple," she stated. "The head masks are really elaborate. Just tell everyone to wear the same colors as their masks. It doesn't have to match perfectly or anything." She saw the flippers John was holding. "Oh, and those. Those are good."

"Thank you, darling," John said. I guessed what everyone's shoe sizes were, and John said he'd get us all flippers.

Carolyn left and reappeared as Dad and I were eating our salads. "You know what? I'll get you some old gardening gloves that we can paint green."

"That sounds great," I said, hoping that Marin would like to help me paint them.

The next day, I called all the people who would be frogs and told them the costume idea. Marin said she would wear a green shirt over blue tights for her red-eyed tree frog. Sarah had brown leggings and a green shirt for her two-headed leopard frog, and she said they would have Julie wear her light green tights and dark green leotard for Frog X. Curt had a yellow shirt and light brown pants for his golden poison frog, and John had dark green pants and a green shirt for his bullfrog. "And don't worry, even though I've joined a gym, I'll probably still have my paunchy tummy for the film shoot, just like a bullfrog," he added.

I realized I needed to write out cue cards for people to read their lines from. Sarah said she would memorize hers and try to get Julie to do the same, but I decided to give everyone the chance to read them if they wanted.

I leafed through the script so far and groaned. How

would I write all of this out by hand? I thought of setting Lenore on the case, making her write everything out on poster board with a smelly marker.

Luckily, when I told my dad that I wanted him to drive me back to the art store for poster paper, I told him why I needed it, and he had a better idea.

"Type your script," he advised. "And then we'll take it to a copy store that makes super-big copies."

"You can do that?" I asked, full of relief.

"Yup," he said. In gratitude, I decided that Lenore could simply hold up the lines for people to read.

Lenore. It was time to call her. I decided to type the script for a while and then call her. I got bored with typing pretty quickly, slid off my chair, groaned, picked up the receiver, and dialed the number I had memorized many years before.

Mrs. Nielson answered, and I asked to speak to Lenore.

"May I ask who's calling?" she asked politely.

I wanted to ask why she cared, but I said my whole name, Amalee Everly, as if she'd never heard of me.

"Amalee?" she asked excitedly. "Hi! It's me, Mrs. Nielson."

She'd never been this nice before. The last time I'd

seen her was over a year ago when I'd gone over to apologize for pushing her daughter down the stairs at school. Phyllis had come with me to let Mrs. Nielson know it was really an accident that had happened after Lenore passed on some gossip she'd heard that my father was dying. By the end of the night, she'd been embarrassed, and I'd felt pretty embarrassed, too.

"Hi, Mrs. Nielson, how are you?" I asked.

"Oh, good, good. Lenore just got back from swimming laps at the pool."

Lenore liked swimming laps, I knew, because she could do it alone. I was probably the last friend she'd had, and now we basically avoided each other. Whenever I saw her, she was alone, clutching her books to her chest the way she had in fifth and sixth grade, even though she wasn't the only girl in our class who wore a bra anymore.

"Swimming laps sounds like fun," I said.

"She's here if you'd like to speak to her," Mrs. Nielson added. "Hey, I heard that you're making a movie. Is that true? I'm sure Lenore would like to help. I mean, love to help. I'm sure she'd *love* to help."

"That's actually why I'm calling," I told her, feeling terrible that I'd tried to come up with the gruntiest grunt job for her lonely daughter, and that the only reason I was calling was that Sarah had already said Lenore could be a part of it. “I wanted to know what she’d be interested in doing.”

“Lenore!” Mrs. Nielson yelled. “Lenore, it’s the phone for you! She’ll be right there, Amalee.”

“Hello?” Lenore asked suspiciously. I tried to remember if I’d ever heard that she’d been the victim of group prank calls at sleepover parties.

“Hi, Lenore, it’s Amalee Ev — it’s Amalee.”

“Hi.” That was all she said.

“Hi, I don’t know if you’d be interested in this at all, but I’m making a short film this summer about endangered species, and I was wondering if you’d like to help out on it. It’s not very glamorous, but . . .” I was in a corner. I didn’t want to lie and say I really wanted to see her. I didn’t want to admit that I felt sorry for her, or that I just wanted her for her manual labor. “But it would be nice to see you, and we’d really like the help, if you’re interested.”

“I’m interested in endangered species,” she said in her soft whiny voice. “What would you like me to do?”

“What would you like to do?” I asked.

“I don’t know what I’m good at,” Lenore answered quietly. “I could carry stuff, if you like.” This was not the Lenore I had known in sixth grade.

"Well, I was wondering if you could be there when we're shooting the narrators, five people who will be dressed like frogs. It's a pretty tough job, because their lines will be on big paper, and you'll need to know when to go to the next cue card so they know what to say next."

"I could glue the paper onto boards," Lenore suggested. "And write the last few lines of each page on my side of the board so I would know when to go to the next one."

"That's really smart," I said. "I hadn't thought of that. That would work." I bet she hadn't heard a compliment in a long time. She always gave them to herself by telling me how well she did on tests and how she always chose the most difficult school projects.

I told her which days we'd be shooting. She paused as if she were going through her schedule, which was probably nonexistent. "That's fine. I'll be there," she said. "Let me know if there's anything else you'd like me to do."

"I will. Thanks a lot," I said.

"You're welcome. Uh, thank you, too," she said. "Good-bye."

I added her name to the contact list.

I started typing again, full of surprise at how good it felt to have finally spoken with Lenore. About an hour later, the phone rang. It was about four o'clock.

A man's familiar deep voice asked, "Is this Amalee?"

"Yes," I said.

"This is Robert Nurstrom."

"Oh, hi!" I said, which probably surprised him. I was usually pretty shy when we spoke. He had practically lived at our house for a few months when he was treating my dad. Then suddenly he was going out with Joyce, and before I knew it, he was marrying her. I just didn't know how to think of him or what to say to him, but if I could talk to Lenore Nielson, I could handle anyone.

"Hi, Amalee," he said uncomfortably. "Joyce said I should talk with you about medicines that come from the rain forest and their possible connections to endangered species."

"Oh, wow, yeah," I said. "Could we do an interview on film?"

"No!" he cried. Then he cleared his throat. "No, that's, uh . . . we don't *need* to do that. Do we?"

"No, no," I assured him. "Anything is fine. We can talk at the restaurant, or right now."

"I just know what other doctors know. I'm not an expert, but I told Joyce I could point you in the right direction."

"Well, I've got paper right here," I said, running into Dad's room to get some paper.

Dr. Nurstrom went on to give me a treasure trove of

information. He said the poisonous bark from a tree called the various curare lianas was turned into a preparation that was just called curare, and that there was a drug being made without the bark but that had its properties. It was used to treat Parkinson's disease, multiple sclerosis, and muscle diseases. Then he told me about something called quinine that comes from cinchona trees and treats malaria. Like curare, there was now a drug that could be made without using the actual plant. But, he pointed out, there were thousands and thousands of species of plants and animals out there, and these plants gave us examples of how valuable rain forest plants could be, and some were in very unique and fragile ecosystems. He said that there was no shortage of the cinchona trees that gave us quinine, but there was a small flower that was very rare and might have faced extinction before we'd found out the amazing things I could do. He told me to look up the rosy periwinkle from Madagascar.

"You can go online, right?" he asked.

"Sure," I said.

"Go online and look it up. I think it's the kind of thing you're looking for."

And it was. I read all about the little rosy periwinkle, an endangered flower that treated and increased the survival rate for infants with leukemia. This was the reason I was writing the film.

That night, before I went to bed, I said, "Good night, rosy periwinkle. I'm making this film for you and all the kids you saved." I thought of a young nurse named Rosy Periwinkle stealing into the children's hospital and appearing at the side of a few busy-looking doctors as they tried to treat the dying children.

"I think I could help, if you let me," she said quietly.

"Go ahead. We've tried everything else," they said, stepping aside.

Rosy Periwinkle smiled as she took a child's hand, knowing that she would make all the difference in the world.

✿ CHAPTER FIFTEEN ✿

The Final Touches

The next day, thanks to even more constant rain, I finished typing the script.

In the middle of the day, I also made popcorn and watched a film called *Medicine Man* that Joyce had rented for me, which I loved, considering that it had to do with a doctor living in the rain forest and learning about the medicinal plants from the people who lived there. It felt great to kick back, space out, watch a movie, and call it "research."

I ran out to get the mail in the afternoon, when the weather had cleared. Along with the letters, there was a bundle of old gardening gloves in all sizes. There was no note, which meant it was from Carolyn. I didn't see anything small enough for Julie, but I thought we'd manage.

I couldn't help peeking down the road. There was Kyle, sitting alone on his front porch, eating an apple with one hand and waving to me with the other. I was suddenly gripped with the idea that he looked over at my driveway as much as I looked over at his, but my excitement was replaced by panic. Should I go over?

"Hi, Amalee, how's it going?" he yelled.

I ran over to him, just to spare his vocal cords.

"Oh, hi. It's good. Things are good."

"What are those in your hands? Gardening gloves?"

I looked down. "Oh, these. These are gardening gloves, yes. See, the movie is going to have people dressed as frogs, and the frogs are going to explain why it's important to save the endangered species."

"That's really cool," he said. "I was wondering how you were going to make it funny."

"Your girlfriend didn't think it was possible," I pointed out. "I can see why it would be confusing." I added this in case he thought I was openly suggesting that his girlfriend was the problem, not my film.

"I *knew* you could pull it off if that's what you decided to do," Kyle told me.

So did this mean they'd broken up?

"Well, we'll see."

"Let me know when it's done." Kyle stood up. "I'd like to see it."

So did this mean they'd broken up?

I walked home telling myself, again, that it didn't matter if my sixteen-year-old neighbor had a girlfriend or not. He was too old.

I called Sarah and Marin and asked if they wanted to come over and paint gloves with me.

Lydia said that Sarah couldn't come to the phone, because she was "a prisoner of her own boredom." I heard Sarah calling out in the background, "Save me! Save me!" Then she came to the phone and said she'd paint a *house* if it would give her something to do. I told Sarah I'd just seen Kyle alone, and she asked if that meant he'd broken up with his girlfriend. I said I couldn't tell. She asked me why I hadn't asked!

Lydia said she'd drive Sarah over in a few minutes. I made more popcorn.

Marin's mother dropped her off in a big black SUV with dark windows. Elegant, yet gloomy. Sarah showed up a little later. I was really happy to see both of them. I told them about Lenore and how she was going to hold the lines for everyone. They both felt bad for her, especially to hear that she had become so quiet and shy.

"She was always so into complaining or boasting. I can't imagine her sounding like a big deflated balloon," Sarah said.

"This is good," Marin said. "She's like a misfit, and we have a place for her."

"Yeah, it's a good thing," I said, smiling at Sarah to let her know I was giving her the credit.

These were real friends. I felt like Lenore when I was in sixth grade, always slinking around feeling like no one liked me. Marin and Sarah were the kind of the people who would want me to feel better. I felt lucky that I found them, which also made me feel more generous toward Lenore.

We got out the frog books, and Marin got excited about painting all the round, suction-cupped toes. Sarah and I just painted the gloves green or yellow, depending on the frog.

When Sarah and I were done with our part, she asked, "So, can I see this script?"

"Oooh," I groaned, "I didn't think it was bad until you just asked."

"Stop!" she ordered. "I know it will be great. And I have another idea. Since two of the frogs are right here, why don't we call up Curt and have a play reading?"

"A play reading?"

"Or, you know, a script reading. It gives us a chance to try our lines, and you a chance to hear how they sound. It's really useful." She tried to read my mind. "Curt is really a nice person. He won't make fun of you. And *we* won't make fun of you."

"Just you and Marin," I told her.

Sarah nodded. "But if it's good," she bargained, "we're calling him. We've got to fit him for his mask and gloves, anyway." She had a point.

The problem with Curt was that I couldn't tell where he stood. I'd seen him with popular kids, because he liked to play sports, but he was such a monkey that everyone liked him, including the teachers. He had no fear. When you're a person like that in our school, you stand out. He played soccer and he'd tried out for the school play. And he was pretty good-looking, though not as gorgeous as Kyle.

"We'll see," I bargained back.

We sat with Marin while she painted the designs on the gloves.

"Dang, you are good!" Sarah commented.

"Thank you," Marin muttered as she drew a curvy dark green ridge across the back of a glove. Then she looked up. "Tell me how the movie is going while I paint these. I shouldn't talk too much."

I launched in about the tai chi people, Gail at the Hall of Biodiversity, Henry at the aquarium, Betsy at the nursery, editing with Phil, and the phone call I had with Dr. Nurstrom. They were both impressed. I had to admit to myself that I had gotten a lot of information. I added that we were going to see Julie's dance, too.

"Oh, yeah, that reminds me," Sarah said. "Ms. Farraday wants you to come to the actual stage to see how it's all going so you know where to stand and all that. She said no pressure, she just thought it would be helpful."

It *would* be helpful. The performance was on Friday, so I would go the day before. Sarah also invited us to a cookout just outside of Woodstock for the Fourth of July on Sunday. She said I could bring my dad and his "little playmates." We all laughed.

Marin asked, too casually to be casual, "Hey, I was wondering if you've found out anything more about your mother."

Sarah raised her eyebrows, opened her mouth, closed it, and looked at me expectantly.

"I have," I started. I felt nervous. I'd never said big things about anyone I was related to, or even about Dad's friends. But these were my friends. Not Dad's friends who were also my friends. These were real friends. You could tell secrets to your friends. That's what girls did, right?

"I found out why everyone always said she was pretty crazy, and like a child, and all that."

"They did?" Sarah asked. "I didn't know that. Actually, though, I asked Lydia about your mom once." Lydia worked at SUNY New Paltz with Dad, and I knew they ran into each other sometimes. "She said your dad said he was very young when they were together, and that she was a lot of fun, and he wished she had lived longer so she could have finally grown up, so I guess he was saying she was kind of . . . young, but not in a bad way."

"No, not in a bad way," I said, thinking of teachers we had who acted young and were fun, like our gym teacher and our hippie music teacher. They were young in a good way. Then I thought of Sally and said, "She was young, not in a bad way, but in a sad way."

"Well, yeah, she passed away," Sarah said.

"But also, the thing was, as it turned out, she was a pretty serious alcoholic," I said. "She was drunk when she got in the car accident that killed her."

Marin stopped painting for a moment. "Huh. My grandfather was an alcoholic. And it *is* sad. He died pretty soon after I was born. My mom said he was awful when he drank."

"I guess when my mother was drunk, she was fun," I said.

"But it's still sad," Sarah noted. "I can't believe they didn't tell you sooner. That's such a big deal."

"Well, you know how my dad has such close friends? I think they're like, 'You don't have to think about that person called Sally, because we can take care of you, so you don't have to worry about not having a mother.' " I thought of Phyllis. They also didn't want me to worry that I'd end up like her, so they showed me I could be like them instead.

"That's really sweet of them," Sarah said. "They are such funny people. I can just see them trying to pretend that they just happen to be four parents instead of one. But actually, that's like Lydia. She's like, 'Don't worry that your mom is so wound up that she can't even look you in the eye and her cell phone rings every five seconds. You've got me, and I'm totally into hanging out!' "

Sarah and I disappeared into the kitchen and made cinnamon toast for the three of us.

"Hey, did you ever go back and listen to that tape of your grandmother?" Sarah asked.

"Oh, I've been meaning to do that! I haven't even listened to hear if it came out," I said.

“Let’s hear it now,” Sarah said. I led her into Dad’s room and got his tape player.

“I’m sure my voice sounds totally weird,” I warned her. “You know I was really nervous about being there.”

“Turn it on!” Sarah ordered.

I rewound a little and pressed PLAY. My grandmother was saying, “And what do you like to do?”

“I like history, and reading — well, English in general — and riding my bike, and science,” my voice answered. Wow, did I sound nervous! But Sarah wouldn’t let me turn it off.

“Is that her breathing?” Sarah asked. We couldn’t tell. There was more silence. I apologized to Sarah. “I was tongue-tied. I wasn’t such a great interviewer. I felt like when I asked big questions, she thought I was pointing out that she was about to die, as if I was saying, ‘Is there anything you’d like to say, now that you’re on your deathbed?’ ”

“She *was* on her deathbed. Maybe she was relieved.”

“Do you think you could have asked those questions to a person you’d never met before?”

“I think I could have, but my dad says that it’s a blessing and a curse the way I blurt things out sometimes. When I was eight, I asked my great uncle when he’d started wearing a wig. And my father jerked his head around, and I said, 'I'm sorry, I mean, when did you start wearing a *toupee*?' It was awful."

I slipped the tape out of the tape player and put it on my desk. I decided to listen to the whole thing in the next few days. Sarah and I went back to the kitchen to get the toast, and Dad came home a few minutes later.

"Hiya, girls," he called out. He squatted next to Marin to see how her painting was going. "That's excellent," he observed. "I'm really impressed with your work." That was my dad. He encouraged everyone. I felt like my house was a safe harbor for Marin, and I loved my dad for that.

"You girls want to stay for dinner?" he asked. Sarah and Marin both called home and got permission to stay. It was Friday, the most crowded night at John's restaurant, so we always ate at home. Friday was becoming easy pasta night at my house. "The more famous John becomes as a chef, the less I remember how to cook!" Dad once complained.

We all laughed when Phyllis showed up about fifteen minutes later, followed by Carolyn. They'd forgotten how to cook, too. Carolyn brought her own homegrown lettuce and snow peas, and Phyllis brought tomatoes, as well as wine for the adults and soda for us.

We all spent the next half hour chopping and stirring, and when we all sat down, Phyllis raised her glass and surprised me by saying, "To Amalee and her friends and their big movie!" I had forgotten about the movie. I was thinking about my grandmother. It was dawning on me that she'd said some pretty important things. I'd definitely have to listen to the tape again.

✿ CHAPTER SIXTEEN ✿

Flippers and All

The Fourth of July was a blast. We all ended up walking about a mile in the dark to get to a hill where we watched a big fireworks display. Sarah insisted that I film the fireworks. They looked like flowers to me. I wondered how they'd come out. When we drove home, I saw Kyle's car in the driveway and felt a little excited. Sarah had given me the idea that if he liked girls who liked science, maybe he could overlook my age. It was a long shot, but I couldn't just look at his car and give up hope.

When I got home, I plugged the camera cable into the television set to see if the fireworks had come out. The white ones had. I was sure I could use them somewhere in the movie. Everything was about the movie these days. Everything felt like it was connected to everything else, just like the woman in my dream had said.

I asked John if he thought about preserving ecosystems when he bought all the food for his restaurant. He shook his head and laughed, "Stop thinking so much or your head will be as big as a basketball!" But then he said, "I don't have to think about ecosystems, Ama, honey, 'cause I grew up in the South. They teach you to be proud of your food there, and how foods from the same land belong together, so I'm always getting stuff that comes from where we live. There's a great mushroom farm and world-renowned apple orchards nearby, and during hunting season, I get deer for venison. In May, I put fiddlehead ferns in the salads that I pick in the woods myself. The more your food is local, the better, I think. The more it tastes like home. The ingredients fit together because they've grown next to each other. Except for wine. Our local wine really stinks. I get most of ours from France, but it's from a river valley not unlike our own river valley. And I try to buy wine from families who have been in business for centuries."

He went on and explained, "Some family businesses are like endangered species. They pass ancient knowledge along through the family line, and if the family business ends, the knowledge becomes extinct. But if you keep the business alive, it survives, and you can taste all that history and knowledge in whatever they create."

John was adding on a whole new layer of everything being related to everything. Unfortunately, I didn't have a basketball of space in my head to take it all in.

"Oh," he said, "and here are the flippers. Next Wednesday is fine for the big shoot. I can't wait."

"How's Frederick?" I asked.

"Oh, you should ask him . . . or his boyfriend." John groaned quietly. "I had no idea he was already spoken for, as they say."

Hoping to make John feel better, I said, "That happened to me, too."

"Oh, no — already it begins?" he sympathized, giving me a hug. "I'll tell you, heartbreak is one creature you can't kill with a stick or a silver bullet. It'll never be extinct." He sighed and released me. "Well, see you on Wednesday, flippers and all."

On Monday night, I dropped the script off at Curt's house. He answered the door himself. He was more handsome than I remembered. He looked like he'd been running around outside. "You're the last one to get it, but no one's told me what they think of it yet," I said. "I hope you don't think it's totally awful."

"I'm sure it's okay," he said shyly. I wished that we'd gotten around to the script reading that Sarah had suggested. I had no idea if it was any good, and here was this kind of popular kid who was better-looking than I'd thought, which shouldn't have made me feel more anxious, but it did.

"It's not this Wednesday, but the one after that, right?" he asked.

"Two o'clock," I said.

"I'll be there, with my brown pants and yellow shirt," he said, smiling. "Why couldn't I have been the one with the two heads?" he asked.

"Sarah got first dibs," I said. "I know what you're going to say: She *always* gets to be the pretty one."

Curt laughed. "Remember when she walked around school with that gray dye in her hair? That was cool."

Good for him. I'd think most boys would say another word besides *cool* — like *uncool*, for instance. I felt better about leaving my script with him as I biked away. I came home to a message from Sarah saying she probably couldn't memorize all the lines, but she was trying, and she was working hard with her sister, who couldn't really read. The next message was also from her, almost shouting.

"By the way — this script is fabulous! Did Curt like it?" Then she hung up, and my heart lifted. I felt both embarrassed and proud. I called to see if she wanted to go on a bike ride, but she said she was going to flatten boxes at Green Pastures to make a little money.

"I had a question while I was going through my lines, though," Sarah said. "How are you going to hear our voices through those masks? Won't they be muffled? And if you put mikes up inside the masks, won't that sound funny, too?"

There were Ellen and Hallie, shaking their heads in my mind. *"Wellllll?"* they asked.

Sarah said, "Uh-oh. Did I just open a can of worms? Look, I'll ask my dad, and you ask your dad."

"You're not going to ask Lydia?"

"If you really needed a barrel of organic brown rice, Lydia would be helpful," Sarah said in explanation. "Sound systems and electronics are the stuff of Ed Smythe."

Dad had a "semi-emergency" rule about calling him at work. He said it didn't have to be an emergency, just important. I called and told him I had a perfect semi-emergency. He called back in a few minutes.

"There's no way I can get the right sound for everyone's voices if they're in those masks," I explained.

"Whoops! Hadn't thought of that," Dad answered cheerfully. I calmed down a little.

"Do we need some kind of expert to get the

microphones positioned?" I asked, thinking of thousands of dollars.

Dad said, "No, no. Wait, I have an idea. Let me make a phone call."

He called back a few minutes later and said, "There's a new guy in the audiovisual department. He said, for a hundred dollars, he would sit everyone down in front of microphones in a studio here and they could say their lines. Then you could have the frogs act along with their lines at the shoot. Do you get what I'm saying?"

I thought of the frogs gesturing along with lines, like a cartoon. It's not like you could see their mouths moving in the masks, anyway. "That would work," I agreed.

"Ned's a great guy. I wouldn't mind having an excuse to hang out with him." Ned was the audio guy. "He actually said he'd do this for free. I insisted on paying him."

"That's fine. We have the money," I said.

"Excellent. Ned believes this is a better way to go with the film, anyway, if you're going to be editing in and out the frogs but still using their voices as you cut to pictures and stuff. He said it would be much cleaner."

I called the frogs and found out that everyone could record their lines in a couple of days. We'd just have to go early in the morning so John could get to the restaurant.

At eight thirty on Thursday morning, we were all a little groggy. Sarah's dad drove Sarah, Marin, and Curt, while John drove with me and Dad. All the men nodded to each other in the parking lot, and they all had large cups of coffee. Dad had a travel mug, which he'd been using religiously ever since I'd asked him about what he'd done for endangered species. Ned came out of the building and shook everyone's hand. He looked familiar, but I couldn't figure out why.

Sarah came right over to me and said, "We have a little problem. Julie chickened out. She says she can do the movie, but she was too nervous to say all the words. She hasn't been reading very long."

"Oh, boy," I answered. I looked at our other choices. Dad and Ed Smythe and me. "I'll do it," I said.

"I'm so sorry. Julie said she was sorry, too. I could do it, but I was thinking it would be better if you did it."

I looked at Sarah. "No, it would be better if you did it," I said. "You don't have to sound like a different person, but you should do it." I felt silly for forgetting that these were voices, and that Sarah could do two of them and no one would know. "I think you're a great actress, and you already said you went over the lines with your sister."

"I almost memorized them myself," she admitted.

"I've got you all set up," Ned announced, springing along through the parking lot and leading us into the studio, which was nice and cool.

Sarah's dad said he'd be back in a couple of hours.

Everyone sat in solid, squeak-proof chairs. Ned took everyone's vocal level. I'd placed the scripts on music stands, opened to each actor's lines.

The recording began. John was very casual and didn't get every word right, which was perfect for everyone's mood. Sarah, Marin, and Curt loosened up when they saw they could fudge a little. And whenever they made a big mistake, they simply started their sentences again, just like John had done.

I nodded to Dad when we got to the end of each script sheet I was holding, and he silently took them from me. About halfway through, when John was starting a sentence again, Dad offered to take over for me, and we switched roles.

At the end of the round, Ned's voice came out of the control room and said, "Since it's only about thirteen minutes of script, why don't you do it all again?"

"A little more coffee, and I'm game," John called out to the invisible voice.

"Dude! You don't have to shout into the mike!" Ned told him from the control room.

"Sorry, bullfrogs are known for their resonant, boomy voices," John said at room level, "and for their cinnamon biscuits." He went to his knapsack and pulled out a big bag. "Amalee, you'll have to excuse the cinnamon. It is not from the Hudson Valley."

"I'll eat hers if she has a problem with that!" Sarah offered. Sarah was John's biggest fan.

After biscuits and trips to the water fountain and to the bathroom, we started again. The whole thing took about sixteen minutes with hardly any mistakes. And everyone sounded better, too. Curt and Marin had improved, and Sarah, who had been fine on the first round, had a little more feeling in her voice without overdoing it. What was really amazing was how she did Frog X the second time. Maybe she was bringing in some of her grandmother's voice. Or even my grandmother's voice. It sounded very steady, but also papery — not sandpapery, just dry. It was as if Frog X knew the ways of us humans and decided long ago not to beg for anything. Frog X just wanted to state her case. I felt the tightening in my throat again, and felt protective of Frog X and sorry for a world that didn't know how to save its own creatures.

When it was all over, Curt told Sarah, "I like the way you made those two frogs sound different." Sarah said she liked the way he didn't sound like he was boasting when he talked about how poisonous he was. We all laughed at that.

Ned came out and started taking down the microphones. "Very interesting stuff, Amalee. My sister is totally into all of this. She's going to love this." I thanked him and asked, looking at my dad first to see if I was going too far, how he would recommend I edit the voices.

"I edited as we went along," he said. "The second performance is clean. I took out all the mistakes. And I'll give you a digital file of the first performance. If you want to edit any of that stuff in, call me, and I'll help you out. In fact, I'd be happy to help you when you do the filming. This is all my bag, you know. It's what I do."

I looked at my dad again and then at Ned. "I'll pay you another hundred dollars for your help," I offered. "I would love it if you were there."

Ned laughed. I thought I knew that laugh. "How about you pay me in biscuits?"

"How about I pay you with dinner at my restaurant?" John asked. "Plus biscuits."

It was settled. Ned would join us next Wednesday for the big shoot. I told all the frogs how happy I was with what they'd done. As we drove home, John and Dad both said they were proud of me.

* * *

The next week I spent deciding exactly what I wanted to pull out of each person's interview. I reviewed what I'd already decided and added and subtracted some lines. I also made a lot of cookies, popcorn, and cinnamon toast and took some bike rides. This was definitely the most boring part of making a movie.

On Tuesday morning, I ran around calling everyone to confirm the time for Wednesday. Lenore was going to paste the big script paper onto the paper boards I'd gotten for her. Mrs. Nielson would come by and pick everything up. We decided we should still have a script for the frogs to play along with. They would come to the dance building at noon the next day. Lydia would bring Sarah and Julie a little early to get Julie used to us. They said she was feeling nervous, which made me nervous! Curt, Sarah, and Marin said they were all set.

John would be coming at around ten in the morning with coffee, scones, and a tray of whatever was left from the night before at the restaurant.

"And my hair and makeup people are arriving at the same time," he joked. "They do *all* my movies."

"And do we need to bring anything special for Phyllis and Carolyn?" I asked.

"Actually, their names are Phyllis and *Joyce*," he said

drily. "Carolyn is the celebrity hairdresser of plants, not humans."

Joyce was also bringing brownies and said that she and my dad would hold lights and help set anything up if I needed it. The room had a little skylight, and the walls were white, so I thought we'd probably use the lightbulbs in the room and be fine. I'd filmed a little when I first checked out the room, and now I was happy to have gotten that professional responsibility out of the way.

I read through the script again in the afternoon. I planned out what I'd do with the camera for each of the lines.

Then I set aside a big pile of camera stuff to bring to the shoot, plus the painted gloves, extra green shirts, tights, pants, and a couple of Dad's big green shirts, just in case. I left the things for Lenore in the front hall before Lydia picked me up to go watch the rehearsal for Ms. Farraday's dance class.

Ms. Farraday led me around the stage before the rehearsal began and showed me places from which she'd recommend shooting. "For the butterflies, I'd say you should be right in the front. I'll set aside a seat for you. And for the ocelots, I put a little stepladder right here on stage left so you can be slightly above them, and then for swamp panther, I'd recommend off to the side on the floor. It's very short, and it's just three girls. Do you have a friend named Hallie?" Without looking at me, or the shocked look on my face, she continued, "Her sister Anna is one of the panthers. In fact, she's coming early to practice her part. The whole thing about these black panthers is that they're hard to see, so they'll be weaving in and out of big plants. So I'd kneel down just below the edge of the stage there, so you can catch them at a diagonal." This was very exciting. Ms. Farraday was speaking to me as if I was a professional filmmaker.

"Hello? Is this the stage?" a familiar voice called into the room. In walked Hallie, holding her sister Anna's hand. Her eyes widened when she saw me, and then she looked down at the floor for an instant.

"Hi, Amalee," she said finally.

"Hi, Hallie," I answered.

"You know each other, right?" Ms. Farraday asked.

"Yes," I said.

"Yes, and I hear you're making a film," Hallie offered in a friendly voice. "Do you need any help?" She looked like she was holding her breath.

I couldn't say no. How bad could it be for one day? And I couldn't deny that she seemed different when she was helping her sister get to dance class instead of standing silently next to Ellen as she pointed to girls who didn't brush their hair correctly.

"We might need some help," I said. Ms. Farraday looked confused that we weren't more comfortable with each other. "We're filming the narrators of the film tomorrow, and — they're frogs — and it should be pretty busy. I'm sure we'll need help with costumes and . . . things like that. It's right in this building, in Room One-fourteen."

Hallie said she would come in the late morning. I figured everyone else would be there in the late morning, too, and they'd protect me if Hallie made one of her zinger comments.

The other young girls had arrived. "All right, then," Ms. Farraday said, "shall we get a rare glimpse of the graceful swamp panther?" The three girls pulled out black tights and sweatshirts with panther ears on the hoods.

Ms. Farraday provided four green cartoonish plants. "They're my sofa cushions," she explained. I saw that she'd gathered in the sides and tops at different angles with green thread to turn the rectangular pillows into odd plant blobs. She placed them on the stage.

Hallie's sister Anna came up beside me and asked, "You're making the movie about endangered species?"

"That's right," I said. "Is that an important thing to you?"

"Yes," she answered with the same quiet seriousness that Hallie had. Then she jumped up onto the stage — like a panther, I thought.

Ms. Farraday talked the dancers through the piece. I could tell that the girls had become panthers the same way they had become monkeys in class. I couldn't take my eyes off them.

Ms. Farraday said not to worry about seeing all the dances now. She said she felt confident I would get what I needed by filming from the angles she suggested.

And so I went home. We went to the restaurant that night, and John showed me that he'd found a light green shirt and a darker green shirt to go over it.

"It's just an option," he said, as if I was a stern director who might yell at him for the suggestion. "We can nix it if you want. I just thought this would give the appearance of a lighter underbelly."

I told him we'd look at it with the mask and decide.

Carolyn appeared beside me at the table and looked at John's choices of shirts. "I'll help you with costumes tomorrow," she offered. "And I have something from Betsy, who sends her best wishes."

Was that the moment that I realized tomorrow was

almost here? It wasn't such a big deal, I'd thought, but now it seemed huge!

I went home and put out a few other things that I thought would be helpful, like the frog book, the mask book, and a couple of desk lamps to add extra light if we needed it. I looked at the pile of stuff. Dad came by and said, "Looks like you're ready to go."

It looked like the kind of pile a person puts together when she has no idea what she's doing. *Maybe that's what Sally's blood is for*, I thought, *to just go ahead and leap*. Like a frog, flippers and all.

CHAPTER SEVENTEEN

Lights . . . Camera . . . Animals

I set my alarm for eight a.m. I woke up at six thirty. When I opened the refrigerator, I saw a big bowl of fruit salad that Dad had obviously stayed up to make. I could imagine him thinking he had nothing to offer except his ability to drive me to the set and then deciding to chop up some fruit as his humble gift. I had some, along with as much cereal as I could eat, which was only a mouthful.

When I heard Dad stirring, I made his coffee. John had taught me how to make the perfect cup. I even heated up some milk. "Thank you for the fruit salad," I said, handing him his mug. "You didn't have to."

Just as I'd guessed, he shrugged and said, "I couldn't think of what else I could give you today."

"You gave me my sane blood," I told him.

"Your what?" he asked. "Good coffee, hon."

"Sally had crazy blood and you have sane blood. And I have both," I explained.

"You know, I think she would have been astounded by you," Dad said, without commenting on my comment. He didn't judge. "And she would have loved to be here today. She would be very proud of you." This was one of the first times he'd ever put my mother and me in a sentence together. It made us related, and it was hard for both of us to talk about that.

"Well, I'm glad," I said, unsure of how to tell him how much I wished she could be here now that he'd put the picture in my head.

We headed off for the movie set with the big pile of things I hoped would get us through the day, plus the fruit salad.

We got everything loaded into the room by ten. As I was setting up the tripod, John arrived with two big trays of food. He had a girl assisting him, balancing two aluminum trays of biscuits and scones. It was Hallie.

John cocked his head toward her. "I snagged this little helper in the parking lot," he said. "She's very helpful. I'll keep her!"

John was exactly the kind of person I would have tried to keep away from Hallie, afraid that she'd observe that he was too talkative, too bald, or just . . . too much. But she seemed to love him. “Should I get that coffee machine, John?” she asked quietly. It was her voice, but without any tinge of warning that she was about to be mean.

“Hm. How ’bout you get that tray with the silverware and stuff? The car’s open.”

“Sure. Hi, Amalee,” she said. “This is exciting.” She disappeared.

“What a sweetie,” John said, and I shuddered in spite of myself.

Phyllis and Carolyn started dragging in five beautifully painted chairs whose backs were made of solid wood. Each chair had a different theme painted on the wood. One was all pond colors with a lily pad painted on the back. Another was bright green with a stripe of light blue and orange here and there. Another was spray-painted gold with bright green leaves. The fourth had pond colors, but there were dark green forest trees peeking in from the sides. Minnesota trees, I guessed.

I couldn’t stop staring at the fifth chair, though — the chair for Frog X. It was just green, with gold stars painted around the edges. The other chairs looked like they were impatiently waiting for their frogs to sit on them, but this chair actually looked lonely. I thought of Dad talking about my mom this morning, about how she would have loved to have been here today.

Phyllis and Carolyn noticed that I wasn't smiling. "This is the gift from Betsy," Phyllis said. "She saw the chairs at a tag sale, and she took Carolyn to look at them for the frogs. Did we go overboard?"

Carolyn looked nervous — at least for Carolyn — as she explained, "We tried not to make them too elaborate. We don't want to upstage the narrators. I don't think we did. Are you worried?"

"They're wonderful," I assured them. "They're perfect."

Joyce showed up ten minutes later with a plate of brownies. "Snazzy chairs!" she exclaimed. "Oh, fruit salad!" She set down the brownies and served herself a bowl of fruit. Then she had a couple of scones and some orange juice. "These are heavenly scones, John!" she said.

"No, not from heaven. All the ingredients are local, in honor of our Hudson Valley ecosystem," John corrected her earnestly.

I was busy looking at the magnificent chairs through the movie camera, making Dad sit in each of them with the matching frog masks in front of his head. The masks matched the chairs without looking like they were disappearing into them, especially if I filmed at a slight angle. Also, I was pleased to see that when I pulled the chairs out from the wall and hid a couple of lamps on the floor behind them, the already light wall became an empty, washed-out screen of white, like we were all floating along on a cloud.

With that more or less set, I got the sound ready. I hooked up the CD player and speakers and tried the first CD we'd made with everyone's voice. A new track would start after each person spoke. Each track was less than a minute. If things went smoothly, we could keep going, and if someone messed up, we could just go back and redo his or her part. Everyone liked the idea that this was like lip-synching a music video, but without the lips.

The voices sounded clear and "clean" as Ned had said. I looked at the five noble frog thrones as I listened to each frog talking about the environment, and felt the same thrill Sarah must have felt onstage. Mr. Chapelle would approve of how much the sound of these voices, and even the positions of the chairs, were telling the story.

Ned arrived and confirmed that everything was in place. He pulled out a portable stereo and plugged everything into it. "The sound is a little better on this one. They'll hear it better through those cool masks." I was very glad he was here, just in case there was a problem. He took a peek at the room through my camera as if he and I were director-partners. "Oh, great, great," he murmured. "Those chairs against the bright white background. Very dreamlike." Dad came over and took a look, too. He said it was very sophisticated.

"Hey, stop making me so un-nervous!" I complained. Dad and Ned laughed.

Lenore arrived with her mother. She jumped when she saw Hallie at the food table, laughing with John. I wanted to reassure her that Hallie was behaving better than when she was with Ellen, but Lenore seemed so nervous, I didn't think anything I could say would help.

Marin and Sarah arrived before noon. Marin shot a look at the chairs and looked over at Carolyn and Phyllis. Phyllis gave her a thumbs-up. "You were a part of this?" I asked Marin.

"We did them outside Carolyn's gardening store," Marin said. "Carolyn taught me a lot of new things. I'd never painted furniture before." Carolyn was making sure Marin had an adult artist to show her the ropes. Phyllis was nodding with approval that this "plan," probably her idea, had worked.

No wonder the chairs matched the masks so well. "They are incredible," I said. "You have to pick one out to keep after the shoot!" I imagined everyone in Marin's family staying out of her room because the wild chair colors would be too much for them.

Lydia came in, holding Julie's hand.

"We have some bad news," Sarah said when she got a chance.

"Julie's just going to watch," Lydia said gently. I noticed that Julie had been crying.

Sarah added, "We told her she didn't have to be a frog if she didn't want to be." Marin looked worried.

I knew better than to show my panic. Julie looked like a tiny wreck. Who would be Frog X? Not me, obviously. I looked at Hallie. I looked at Lenore. I looked at Phyllis and almost laughed. Phyllis could not be a frog. Lenore's mother was helping Lenore put the boards in order. She looked up now and said, "Lenore can be a frog if you need her to."

I also knew better than to groan.

Joyce approached Julie with a few brownies on napkins. "Do you think you could watch and eat a brownie at the same time, Julie?" She handed brownies to Lydia, Sarah, and Marin. "How do you like those spiffy chairs?"

"They're pretty," Julie whispered, taking the brownie.

I pulled out a long-sleeved green shirt and green leggings for Lenore to look at. "Try these on, Lenore," I said, hoping that she wasn't horrified that her mother spoke up.

"Are you sure?"

I looked at Julie and said, "I was feeling bad, because I knew the gloves and flippers would be too big for you. Maybe they'll fit Lenore." I nodded to Lenore, as if to say, *The easier you make this, the better it will be for Julie.* I didn't want to beg Lenore to be Frog X. Frog X was very special, and the truth was, I was really upset that Lenore was going to play her, but that's what had to happen.

"Maybe she's like a frog Cinderella. The flippers will fit and reveal that Lenore was supposed to be Frog X all along," I said into Julie's ear. Julie smiled.

"Hey, Julie," Sarah called to her sister, "you can also be the mask straightener for us, if they get wobbly." Julie frowned. "Or not," Sarah said, putting on her mask. John had disappeared to put on his costume, and he came back looking perfect. He had simple dark green pants with a lighter green shirt, and when he put on his mask, we all laughed. This was my favorite part of theater. John looked like a somewhat tired, older frog, while Sarah looked like a very alert, purposeful frog who was determined not to let her two-headedness get in her way. Marin put on her mask and it looked beautiful with her matching outfit. She looked more delicate, like a frog you could hold in your hand. Curt arrived, already wearing his clothes. He nodded to everyone as I introduced him.

"What a cutie-pie!" Joyce gushed to Phyllis. Curt

pretended not to hear. He sauntered over and put on his mask.

"I'm poison frog! Hi-YAH!" he said, doing a karate kick. Julie ran over and straightened his mask.

"It's my job," she explained, standing on one of the chairs to reach Curt's head.

The masks changed everyone who put them on, and Lenore was no exception. She *was* Frog X. She was the frog who didn't know what to bring to the party and hadn't come with her friends, the shy, nervous frog, the one you might not notice if she disappeared.

"You look great, sweetheart," her mother said encouragingly. Lenore folded her arms and slumped a bit.

"You do," I said. Everyone murmured their approval. "You're a natural, Lenore," I added. "Why doesn't everyone put on their flippers and gloves and we'll see if this works?"

I had everyone sit in full costume on their chairs. Again, I needed to be creative with the camera to make it look just right, but I enjoyed the challenge, and it made for more movement in the film to have each frog shot from a slightly different angle. The way everyone made space for me as I walked around with the camera made it all the more real. I was directing. We were ready to start.

* * *

The movie began with John walking in, waving to the camera and sitting down. Next came Sarah, then Marin, then Curt, and finally Lenore, who walked with the least confidence.

I turned on the CD and each frog stepped forward to "say" the lines. John set the tone by looking completely natural and conversational. There was no hopping. At one point, John leaned up against his chair, looking almost like a college professor who happened to be a huge frog.

Lenore did not walk around, though. She stepped forward and only made little gestures with her hands. She was nervous, but her nervousness was so honest that I didn't stop the camera and ask her to do anything different.

Looking at her, I realized that I had one more reason that we should protect animals from extinction. We shouldn't give up on them. Lenore herself was awkward and nervous and not asking for anything but the right to survive. That's all she'd been doing when I'd seen her over the last year: She was surviving. From what I could tell, she didn't stand out in her classes for being smart. She wasn't an athlete, she definitely wasn't funny, and she probably still wasn't particularly nice, but I wanted her to feel like she fit in the world, because who was I to say she didn't? And who was I to say things would not get better for her?

Everyone asked to start over once or twice. It was easy to do. I took the opportunity to pull the tripod and camera over for a new angle. When we finished, Sarah asked if they could do it again. It was already four o'clock.

I said, "Why don't we take a food break and see how we feel?" I thought of all the camera angles I could do even better and hoped everyone would be up for a second try.

Everyone said they would love to run their parts again, even Curt, who was eating fruit salad with Julie and telling her that he was a Super Villain called Poison Frogman. Hallie talked with Phyllis. Dad asked if I needed anything, like aspirin. The room was air-conditioned, the first shooting had gone well, and so, no, I didn't need an aspirin. "Do you?" I asked.

"Oh. Yeah. I do. Why do I always do that to you?" He went off to get some water.

The second time around, everyone was more relaxed, including me, and besides trying some more interesting angles, like one from above as Marin talked about living in the rain forest (she did camouflage with her chair from this angle, but that seemed perfect for the rain forest), I saw that I could edit in some great moments, like John pretending to kiss Marin, mask to mask, and Sarah touching Curt's shirt and writhing in a pretend death.

We were completely done by seven o'clock. John rushed back to the restaurant, and Dad decided to give him a break by ordering pizzas to be delivered to our house instead of taking us all to John & Friends. Dad grabbed some stuff and went home to greet the pizza person.

Joyce drove me home. "So?" she asked.

"I feel great," I said.

"How did you know I was going to ask you how you were feeling? Are you feeling just great, or are you feeling other things? Are you sad that you've cleared this big hurdle? Did you like hearing the script? Did you like how it was recorded?"

"There were things I would have wanted to change, but the fact that the script was done and I couldn't do anything about it let me focus on the camera part, and I loved that." How else did I feel? "I wish my mother had been there," I said, a statement that had more weight than I'd meant for it to have. "Sally, I mean."

"Oh, I know your mother's name," Joyce said, and then she gave me a huge gift: no more questions. We drove silently until we got home.

It felt weird to have Lenore and Hallie in my house again. Hallie had only been over once, and that time I sensed that she had disapproved of everything from the living room couch to Dad's computer. But now she was sitting and laughing with Curt, Marin, and Sarah. Lenore was sitting with Phyllis and Carolyn, which felt like a good match.

Phyllis was doing her best to make Lenore feel comfortable.

Dad was in the kitchen filling up a cooler of ice for the soda. "That was really fun!" he said. "I can't wait to see how it turns out. You want to show me what you have so far? You need some help?"

"No and no," I answered. "I want it to be a surprise."

"Fair enough," Dad said. "You got that from me, you might say. Oh, but speaking of surprises, Ned is coming over with his sister, who moved up here a few years ago and convinced him to move to New Paltz."

"Okay," I said, thinking that wasn't much of a surprise.

"Do you know what Ned's last name is?" I realized I didn't. Dad told me, "It's Severence."

Out in the living room, we heard Ned's voice saying, "Hi, everyone. Do you know my sister?"

And another voice said, "I know some of you." To Joyce and Carolyn, she said, "Hi, I'm Ann."

Ms. Severence was my sixth-grade English teacher!

And she was my favorite teacher. We'd had a good end of sixth grade, but I'd spent so much time trying to impress her. I still felt tongue-tied around her.

Well, you can't hide out here all night, I thought, pushing myself out of the kitchen.

"Hi, Amalee," Ms. Severence said. She was wearing a long purple dress with sandals and pretty silver earrings. Her long blond hair was swept up in a silver clip, and she looked like one of the women who shopped at Lydia's natural food store. "Congratulations. I hear you wrote a great screenplay." And then she gave me a hug and handed me a small wrapped present. (A hug! I saw Lenore's eyes widen.) Everyone was quiet. "It's not a big deal. I just saw it and thought you'd like it," she stammered, looking around. I unwrapped it quickly to save her some embarrassment. It was a fancy metal pen covered with green frogs. It was perfect.

"It's beautiful. Thank you," I said.

Everyone was looking at the pen. Everyone, that is, except Dad. I looked and saw Dad looking at Ms. Severence, and Ms. Severence looking at him.

"We've met a couple of times," he said. "I'm David."

"I know. Hi, David," she said.

I watched their conversation like it was an Olympic Ping-Pong tournament.

"Would you like some pizza?"

"No, thanks."

"Would you like a glass of wine?"

"That would be great."

"Red or white?"

"Red, thanks."

"It's a merlot."

"That sounds great."

Luckily I realized that I was completely starving. The word *pizza* helped to break my trance. Hallie and Lenore, who had been in the same class with Ms. Severence, couldn't take their eyes off of her, either. Even though she'd loosened up over the year when she was our teacher, we'd never seen her doing things like eating pizza and talking *as a friend* to other adults. And now she was drinking wine with them!

Sarah and Marin admired my pen and asked if I would consider doing another movie with the frogs. Sarah said she would write a fiction movie where a two-headed leopard frog, a golden poison frog, and a red-eyed tree frog were called the Green Avengers who would attack polluters. I said that sounded like a fun idea.

"So, your dad seems to like Ann," Sarah said, nodding in their direction.

"Oh, no . . . she was my English teacher," I explained.

"So?" Sarah asked.

"Leave Amalee alone!" Marin interrupted, laughing and poking Sarah. "How would you like it if one of your teachers liked one of your parents?"

Ms. Severence wasn't just one of my teachers — she was *Ms. Severence*. I always thought of her going home and reading thick books about history and coming up with ideas of how to make things interesting for her students. That's what I loved about her. She seemed so smart. And now I looked at her talking with Dad . . . another person, I now realized, who read thick books and thought about how to make subjects interesting for his students. They both seemed so smart, almost like a club that they couldn't allow me into. Or maybe they could. She was in our house, eating our pizza, with her brother clapping me on the back, congratulating me on pulling off the day of filming.

It was hard to feel left out.

✿ CHAPTER EIGHTEEN ✿

We've Got the Whole World in Our Computer

I woke up the next morning and thought about the parade of friends and former foes we'd had in our living room last night. Phyllis, Dad, and I had cleaned up. Ms. Severence had not been mentioned, to my relief. As I saw the pen that she had given me lying on my desk, I realized that neither my shyness nor the weirdness of the situation kept me from feeling really proud of her present. She had thought about me and understood me. The pen was proof of that.

Later in the day, Lydia picked me up and brought Marin, Sarah, Julie, and me to the swimming hole again. We passed Kyle's house, and Sarah didn't even notice. "I feel sad," she said. "Yesterday was so much fun! Are you going to finish the film soon so we can have a big screening party?"

"First we have Julie's big dance concert," I pointed out. Julie slid down in her seat, but she was smiling. We swam and ate leftover pizza that Lydia had put on a baking pan and left in the sun to see if it would cook. It cooked, but not before it caught a few ants. We just picked them off and ate the pizza, rough wild-blooded girls that we were.

I had an appointment the next day at the film department in New Paltz, thanks to my dad. The dance performance would be my reward for sitting in a dark cave of a room for the day.

Dad introduced me to Sandy and Karim in the film room. He slipped them some money — I'd have to ask him later how much. I could see why they wouldn't want to accept money from a twelve-year-old, even one with as many coins as I'd inherited. They seemed to be doing this out of the kindness of their hearts, anyway.

They looked nervous, though, when they saw all the footage to edit. Then I took out a notepad and showed them I had a very good idea what I wanted where.

"You will become less organized as you get older," Karim said, and Sandy nodded. They were also impressed that I already knew something about film editing on a computer.

Sandy wrote something on a Post-it and stuck it on

the corner of the computer. "This is from your dad," she said. The note said, *Whatever you do is enough.* "Has he ever done this to you before?" Yes, he had. Once he had received a brilliant paper from a student. He said it was imaginative and clear, and it seemed like the student had enjoyed writing it, which made it enjoyable to read. When he asked the student what made this paper stand out from other ones she'd written, she said she'd been so nervous that she finally wrote herself a note that said, *Whatever you do is enough*, telling herself that if she only wrote one of the ten pages she was supposed to write, she'd still get a D instead of an F. Three pages were a C–, she decided as she finished three pages. Eight pages must be at least a B. And then she was done, and she hadn't pushed herself to do it. She'd actually had a good time.

I thought of my mom, growing up in a *Nothing is good enough* house and meeting the *Whatever you do is enough* man. She was lucky, in that way.

"I need that note," I admitted.

"Yeah, we got our work cut out for us," Karim said. "Your dad is a smart guy. He pushes the kids who need to be pushed and lays off the kids who push themselves too hard. I've had him for a few classes and I noticed that."

"I don't know if he's always guessed right," I said, thinking of my mom. I decided to let it go at that. We started at the beginning. They agreed with me that I could put opening credits over some footage I'd caught of the "frogs" doing stretching exercises. Then we cut to the camera focusing on John as the other frogs sat down. I loved seeing how some of my original ideas, like John just walking into the room, were less interesting than the ones with more action, and less funny. Whenever we came to the best editing moment, we were able to fine-tune it pretty fast.

John said the opening lines, and then said that every ecosystem had its own web of life, after which we cut to Gail at the American Museum of Natural History giving her speech about the animals pooping and dying and putting nutrients back in the ground. I had been worried about putting real humans next to the big frogs, but the film seemed to be saying that the humans were in their own world, unbothered by the dramatic larger-than-life amphibians. Also the way Gail talked about "poop" made it clear she wasn't trying to give some big adult science lecture!

We edited back to John, who said he didn't want to show off about his importance, but since frogs live in both the land and water, their health is the best way to know what's going on in the environment, because their survival is the most threatened by pollution on the land or the water.

"For instance," John said, "you can tell by looking at me that my ecosystem is very healthy." He patted his stomach. He'd added that line himself.

"This is going to be good," Sandy said, and I swelled like a bullfrog.

We moved on to Curt, who said that even though we live in a world where we can make clothes, medicine, and even food away from nature and in laboratories with chemicals, we had to admit that since we are part of the complicated life of the planet, we always needed to go to the bigger laboratory of the planet Earth for answers. "Does that sound too stuffy?" I asked.

Karim shrugged. "It helps that we're hearing it from a giant yellow frog."

"Golden," I said, smiling.

We went to Betsy in her tank top, brushing back her silver braid of hair with her bracelet-covered arm as she talked about rain forest plants. And then we had Curt again, talking about medicines we get from the natural world. Betsy's purple tank top against the white orchids and Curt's golden mask against the blurred green of the other frogs in their chairs were beautiful contrasts, while the soft light in the greenhouse and the sunlight in the frog room were very similar. These edits were working.

And then Curt came back and talked more about the

quinine we use to treat malaria, the annatto plant that was used in red makeup and face paint, and the curare bark that was used for many medical purposes. We edited to pictures of each plant, but it was too much, so I just used the annatto plant, which was the most interesting. Sandy and Karim nodded along with my choices.

Then Curt said that animals weren't helpful just for the medicines and makeup they gave us. They could also inspire us.

We cut to the tai chi people looking like cranes. Karim and Sandy agreed that we could spend a full ten seconds on the distant shot, and then another seven seconds — a lot, in movie time — on a close-up of one of the women. The golden light was rich and inviting to look at. We edited to Kevin, the curly-haired tai chi guy, talking about the qualities of each of the animals. It was getting a little long, so we just had him talk about the tiger and the crane, editing each one down to a couple of sentences.

"You don't need a lot of what he's saying to get the point across, do you?" I asked. "I mean, he cares about it so much, a little goes a long way."

"It's very intense, yes," Karim mumbled, leaning over to help me make the cleanest cuts so that Kevin's words would still flow evenly. "Less is definitely more here."

Marin then came in, saying that, as the red-eyed tree

frog with bright eyes, light blue legs, and light green skin, she was one of the best-loved frogs in the world. "I'm here to represent how important the natural world is to us, just because it's fascinating and beautiful." Here, I told Sandy and Karim, was where we'd edit in the footage from the dance concert once I had it. We then returned to Betsy admiring the delicate blossom of the orchid, and then introduced Henry at the aquarium. He was pointing toward the ocean tank, which was teeming with busy fish, plus a stingray going by like a slow-motion butterfly. Both Henry and Betsy seemed to be in awe of what they were observing for us, which, Sandy and I said, gave Marin's point more "momentum."

We all laughed as Sarah then got up from her chair with her hands on her hips, as if to say, *Yeah, yeah, yeah, I've got two heads. You think I hadn't noticed?* She talked about the discovery of the mutant frogs in Minnesota, and how scientists were still trying to figure out which chemicals had done this to them. Then we cut in the actual pictures of the leopard frogs. Here I didn't need a smooth transition. As soon as Sarah had made her point, I made a quick cut to the mutated frogs. Karim looked at their withered extra legs and arms. "Poor little guys," he muttered.

Sarah came back and talked about how mussels can

tell us how polluted water is because they filter so much of it, and then she came back to the mutated frogs and said that if the chemicals we were using could do this to frogs, what were they doing to all the other life in the lakes of northern Minnesota? And even if we didn't care, what were these chemicals doing to humans, especially children?

We had shown why plants and animals were important to us. Now we would get into the part about how they were endangered.

We went back to John, who said that due to the way humans were spreading out and over-harvesting, we were losing big chunks of the food chains. I'd gotten some footage of the young tattooed guy at our local fish store who Phyllis said always talked her ear off about "the politics of fish." The red and black tattoos on his arms as he pointed to the different silver fish in the case were striking. "Great color world," Sandy observed. I liked that expression, *color world*.

The guy at the fish store, Dave, was shaking his head at a pile of white fish. "See that? That's cod from Cape Cod, which they catch responsibly, from what I've heard. You know, I'm really careful about what kind of cod we get, because they, like, totally exterminated the population of cod off of Canada and Maine, not because they killed all the cod itself, but — get this — they went out in these HUGE boats, and they were just scraping the bottom of the ocean to get what they could get. I mean, imagine if someone just came and scraped out all the towns between New York City and Albany. So they totally wipe out the whole sea bottom, the population of plankton and all the tiny stuff that all the sea animals eat, and it works its way up the food chain, so good-bye to little fish and then the cod, not to mention that they were also over-fishing the cod itself. Man! You just don't—" He swore here. We replaced it with a bleep sound that we made with the alarm on Sandy's cell phone. "You just don't *BLEEP* with Mother Nature like that."

"Good example," said Sandy, laughing. "I wouldn't want to date him, but he makes his point well."

"That's because you *have* dated him," Karim pointed out.

"That guy?" I pointed.

"He means guys like him," Sandy explained, rolling her eyes at Karim. "Yes, I'm done with angry tattooed guys for now, thank you."

Marin came next and said, "The word for all the complicated, beautiful things we see in nature is *biodiversity*. Gail works at the Hall of Biodiversity at the American Museum of Natural History. Part of what we're protecting is not just this or that species, we're protecting the whole systems that are interconnected."

Gail talked about how every system became more complex the more you looked at it. Then we cut to Henry and the part of our interview where he talked about how he loved the almost infinite variety of plants and animals, all the colors and shapes that existed in the world. And then we flashed though a bunch of photos that Gail had sent. I'd asked her to send pictures of endangered species I'd learned about from books and museums in the last month. We went fast, fast, fast: Nilgiri tahr, Nilgiri langur, Kemp's ridley sea turtle, desert tortoise, Hector's dolphin, giant panda, snow leopard, humpback whale, seabeach amaranth, gorilla, marine otter, Mexican gray wolf, Oregon silverspot butterfly, Palila finch, cucumber tree, Corroboree frog, manatee, pink sand verbena.

Marin came back at the end of the beautiful pictures. It took a second for the eye to see she wasn't one of the photographs. She said, "All of these are endangered." Sandy gasped.

And then we went to Lenore.

"Wow, who's that?" Sandy asked. "So awkward!"

Lenore held out her palms and shrugged as we heard

Sarah's voice introducing Frog X. "I am here to talk about the importance of keeping the environment safe for every species, even when they're not particularly helpful or interesting to us. Perhaps I am not an important part of a food chain. Maybe I have no medicine to offer, I cannot help you detect an environmental disaster. I am not beautiful. But I have a right to stay a part of this planet."

I had written and crossed out every word of what Frog X said. I looked sideways at Karim and Sandy to see what they thought. I couldn't tell! We stopped the film and went back to Gail, Betsy, and Henry.

Henry, standing in front of the fish tank, said, "I just want to live in a world with an infinite variety of flora and fauna, and rocks for that matter. I want to be on a planet with countless life-forms."

Gail, beaming in her purple sweater at the museum, said, "We'll never perfectly replicate the intricacy of interrelationships that actually exist in a natural system. And yet every level of understanding we reach is really wonderful in and of itself."

Betsy, standing in front of a field of orchids rescued from the brink of extinction, said, "It's not just the beauty of each thing. It's how it all fits together. Stunning.

Ingenious. No artist could have thought of it. We have great ideas. We have beautiful ideas. Nature is *the* greatest idea."

Then Lenore's frog said, "And also, just because I don't seem valuable to you now, you never know. People haven't solved the mysteries of the planet. People don't know what the future will bring. People don't know what they need to survive."

Then we edited to some of the footage from Mr. Chapelle's movie. This was technically Curt's turn to narrate, because it was about the usefulness of an animal, but I didn't want him to feel weird talking about Mr. Chapelle, so I'd let John do it. We watched Mr. Chapelle's son in the water with the therapist and the dolphin for about seven seconds, then cut to the therapist saying how this had helped other autistic kids communicate better, for some mysterious reason. John pointed out that we're still in the process of figuring out whether working with dolphins is a key to helping children with autism. Then he said that while most dolphin species were not endangered, their habitat was always threatened.

Lenore returned and said, "Maybe someone needs the secret language of one animal to speak. Maybe someone needs to channel the power of a tiger to survive. Maybe someone needs the bark of a tree to make the painkiller that works. Maybe someone needs the beauty of a tree frog to live. Or the medicine from the rosy periwinkle."

We edited to a picture of the rosy periwinkle as Sarah's voice continued. Karim showed me how to make it look like a camera was traveling over the picture. He called it "pan and scan." Movement added to the suspense here, as if we were exploring the flower as Frog X talked about it.

"This is the rosy periwinkle. It is endangered. It is small and easy to miss. It only grows in Madagascar. The medicine made from the rosy periwinkle has increased the survival rate of infant leukemia by eighty percent. The rosy periwinkle is rare and endangered. We could have lost it, but because we found it, we have created the medicine that helped eighty percent more babies survive leukemia. We don't know what we need to survive."

I inhaled as Lenore came to the last part of the speech. "But I think my friend, Myrtle, who is herself an endangered green sea turtle, says it the best."

We cut to Myrtle swimming around. "She's going to speak," I explained.

I pulled out the tape recorder and turned it on. Sandy already had a microphone out for the *bleep* sound we'd recorded, so I held up the small tape machine and fed the recording onto the computer. I said as long as we could hear the words, they didn't have to be as clear as the rest of the movie.

"Look at the world and listen to the world," the voice instructed. "We set out to teach everyone our lessons, but we need to be taught ourselves. I've watched closely in recent years. Without exception, I have learned important lessons from everything I have observed, from bees to humans. Unfortunately, I acquired the skill of watching and listening too late in life. I had already overlooked things and sacrificed them forever, losing whatever important wisdom they were sent to give me."

It was my grandmother.

We did a last montage of the tai chi people sweeping up their arms like cranes, Henry imitating a swimming sea turtle, and Gail tipping her head like a slender loris. I would also include footage of Ms. Farraday's dance class when I got it.

Then the frogs held up signs with the words THE END and Myrtle came back again with my grandmother's voice.

"Good luck," she said.

✿ CHAPTER NINETEEN ✿

Rainy Day Frogs

After a quick dinner, we ran off to the dance concert, which, with the stage lights, came off even more beautifully than I had expected. The swamp panthers darted in and out of the green plants. Then came the Karner blue butterflies. Sarah was standing next to me with the camera bag in case there was an emergency. We both gasped when the butterflies went running back and forth, which was hypnotizing enough, but then they turned away from us to spread their wings, which were electric blue with designs made with aluminum foil.

"Smell that?" Sarah whispered. "Fried chicken. I told you!" She was right. If you looked closely, you could also see grease stains on the edges of some of the foil.

The last dance was called "Ecosystem." I loved Ms.

Farraday for this. It wasn't scientific. Sarah told me Ms. Farraday had told the dancers to bring any clothing they had with animal prints on them. She made up a dance based on who had the zebra prints, and who had the leopard spots, snakeskin designs, and fake lion fur. All of the animals ended up dancing together, showing that an ecosystem is really a dance of all different species. If she had tried to show the way an ecosystem really worked, she would have had all the animals eating each other. I was glad she didn't go that way.

I was so tired after the performance that I wanted to leave, but I went up to Ms. Farraday to thank her. She looked past all the parents and asked, "Did you get what you needed?" I gave her an okay sign, and she beamed.

The next morning I held my breath and looked at the film of the dances. Nothing could capture the exact moment when the bright blue butterflies had opened their wings, but I still got a shiver when it happened.

On Monday, I went back and finished the film. I knew I would want to clean it up more, but this would do for now. It was a whole thing, if not a perfect thing.

I waited for Dad to do some office work before we drove home from the second editing session. I called Carolyn from the hall outside the editing room and left a message saying that I wanted her, and her alone, to see the film. I chose her because I knew she would see the movie itself, not me. Just as Carolyn had congratulated Marin on her masks by looking at the masks (she hardly knew Marin was there), she would comment on the film itself. I wanted that.

I sat on a wall near the car and watched the wind blow through the trees and flowers around the parking lot of the campus. What were the names of these trees? What kind of flowers were these? Why hadn't I noticed or cared? Dad came out and drove me home. I told him he still couldn't see the film, and I told him he might have to leave the house while I showed it to Carolyn.

He nodded. "That's brave," he said. He knew Carolyn wouldn't know how to lie if she didn't like it.

Carolyn was at our house reading a book on the front step when we came home. My dad gave her a hug and continued inside. She looked up at me and said, "I was trying to get a look at that cute guy down the street who made you have that bike accident."

It was no use being angry with Carolyn or Phyllis. Or John or Joyce or my dad, all of whom had obviously compared notes about Kyle. I sighed. "His name is Kyle, but he has a girlfriend." She already knew that, didn't she? "C'mon in." I said.

Dad said he would close his eyes and ears in his room if we let him stay in the house.

Carolyn and I sat near the television so we could catch the details. And then for the next seventeen minutes I got to experience my blood rushing up through my body like a continuous fountain. Carolyn watched the whole film without smiling, laughing, talking, or even looking in my direction. She gave no clues. I could suddenly see the places where the edits were messy and the script seemed too serious. Ellen, this time without Hallie, was in my head saying she could have done a much better job.

The film ended. "Who was the turtle voice?" Carolyn asked.

"It's a surprise," I said.

"I liked that part the best," she told me, rising and stretching.

How could I ask her if she thought it was any good or not? I couldn't. I didn't.

"Betsy's cool, isn't she?" Carolyn asked.

"She's totally cool. She gave me this bracelet," I answered, holding out my wrist, hoping my hand wouldn't shake.

"Speaking of which, I've got to get back to work," Carolyn said. "And I need to think about this. Good job, Amalee."

And that was it.

I was a little disappointed. When I felt my disappointment start to grow, I decided to get on my bike and go somewhere. I also decided to show the movie to Sarah. I knew, just because she loved to find something good in everything, that she would probably only say something nice, but I decided I wouldn't mind a compliment or two!

I biked away from Kyle's house. I made myself not look for his truck. Then I looked. It wasn't there. I sighed and kept on riding. There were long grass fields on both sides of me as I biked along, and old, old trees. Betsy was right — it was the way it all looked side by side that was even more beautiful than each part. I decided that I had made the film for myself. If no one else liked it, I would survive. My eyes were opened by making a movie.

I looked at my bracelet again. Betsy had called me "a fellow adventurer and planetary healer." Well, maybe I hadn't done much planet healing, but I was trying.

I came home and called Sarah, still hoping that she could take a look and give the movie a clear thumbs-up or -down. She was home, but she said she couldn't come over, because . . . "Because, okay, I'm sure you knew about this. I'm totally embarrassed, but I found out that

Curt is going to the swimming hole today, and so I'm making Lydia take me and pretend it's a coincidence."

"Curt the frog?"

"Oh, like you couldn't tell! I'm such an idiot. You think I'm weird that I like Curt?"

"No. Do you think I'm weird that I didn't know that you liked Curt?" I asked. Now that I thought about it, I should have guessed. I remembered how gently Sarah had helped Curt with his frog mask.

"Do you want to come with us? You don't like him, too, do you?"

I laughed. She put it right out there, after I'd felt so terrible about being jealous of her. "No way."

"Has Kyle broken up with that icky girl?" she asked.

"I don't know," I answered. "Probably not."

"Do you think I'm an awful friend for not coming over to see your movie? You must be really excited."

"No. I feel bad for not going to swim," I lied as I watched black clouds practically flood into the sky. Did I hear thunder? Obviously Sarah did not hear anything that would get in the way of her plan. I added, "Why don't you and Lydia come to John & Friends for an early dinner? You want to sleep over afterward?"

She said yes, yes, yes. She'd have to talk to someone

about whatever was going to happen at the swimming hole. "And I'd love to see the movie. We'll make popcorn and watch it at midnight," she said.

I told her good luck, and thought of Myrtle wishing us all the same thing.

I usually loved rain, but not when it was destroying Sarah's secret date. An hour later, it really started to pour. At five, Joyce came and picked me up on her way to the restaurant. She met me at the door with an enormous purple umbrella.

"Get in the car!" she yelled, and we both shuffled along under the umbrella like some unusual species of hippopatomus.

"Your dad says you've finished the movie," she mentioned casually. "And you won't let him see it."

"I let Carolyn see it," I said, remembering my disappointment. Sarah had helped me more than she knew by making me all nervous for her and Curt instead of me and . . . me.

We ran into the restaurant and found Phyllis with her calculator. Dad arrived a little later and thanked me for leaving a note that I was already at the restaurant. Carolyn nodded from where she stood in the plants.

Joyce went to the kitchen to talk with John,

something she rarely did, but she had been having strange food cravings, so she was probably asking for an unusual dish.

"Handmade tagliatelle pasta with fresh local tomatoes, basil, and garlic," Joyce announced coming out of the swinging doors. "How does that sound? Pregnant lady likes pasta these days."

A server brought out a big bowl and many plates. Lydia and Sarah arrived, soaking, with a little drenched Julie in tow.

"How did it . . . ?" I asked, but Sarah shook her head. I nodded and found seats for them.

The pasta was amazing. I kept reminding myself that I had made the movie for myself. I tried not to look at Carolyn.

The server came out and said, very seriously, that John had made us a dessert. She took our dinner plates and replaced them with dessert plates. John came through the door with a cake. The cake was green. John's smile was huge. He practically plopped the cake on the table, he was so excited for me to see that he had created a very large, noble green frog with a white underbelly. The frog had a crown and a long red tongue coming out of its mouth, and on the tongue were the words AMA RULES!

Carolyn came over and sat next to me. "I loved your

movie," she said. "I almost cried. I just wanted to think about it before I told you."

"Oh," I said casually. "I thought maybe you didn't like it so much."

Carolyn looked confused. "You couldn't tell? I thought it was amazing."

Joyce squeezed my hand and said, "And if Carolyn says she almost cried, you know I'll be bawling."

Phyllis started cutting the cake. "You did it," she said, shaking her head. "I can't believe it. You had a plan and you stuck to it. I told you who you reminded me of." She winked.

Dad said, "I knew she would do it."

I had become a floating balloon, filled with the helium of relief. They couldn't know this, because then I'd have to admit how worried I had been. I told them that making the film hadn't seemed impossible. "Thanks to you," I pointed out. "And you." I nodded at Sarah. "And you!" I looked at Lydia and Julie.

After the cake, we all loaded into different cars with our soggy sandals and sneakers. Sarah had her things with her, so she came with Dad and me. When we got home and Dad had gone to brush his teeth, she turned to me and said, "Okay, this is what happened. We got there just before it started to rain, and then Curt and his friend and his dad showed up, and Lydia and I were looking like we were going to go swimming, anyway, so I thought maybe he'd decide to go, too."

Sarah said it went like this:

Curt got out of his car and said, "Hi! I think it's going to rain."

And Sarah answered, "Yeah, maybe."

He asked, "You think you're still going to go swimming?"

Sarah said, "I don't know. Did you think you would still go?"

And Curt looked up, saying, "Uh-oh. Thunder. You're not supposed to go swimming when it thunders."

Then Lydia came over and offered to take everyone out for ice cream, but Curt said no, and Sarah didn't know why.

"That's great that Lydia did that," I pointed out. "It would have been much more awful if *you* had asked him and he said no."

"I still feel like a loser," Sarah moaned. "I feel so embarrassed. Do you think he'd ever really be interested in me?"

I told her the truth. "I think you're the best-looking

girl in our class." And then I told her how Curt liked that she streaked her hair gray for the class play.

"He did? That's good," she said.

"When did you start to like him?" I asked. "I had no idea."

"Well, I thought he was really good when he did the audition for the play, but then I realized how much I liked him when I saw that story he did for Mr. Chapelle's class."

"So he liked it when you put gray streaks in your hair, and you liked it when he put brown yarn in his, right?" I asked. Sarah nodded. "You're a perfect couple!" I cried.

"You think?" Sarah asked. "I think he is so gorgeous. Has he had braces? I love his teeth. And he's got beautiful eyes. And you know, it's weird, because he's popular, but he's nice to everyone. I think that's really cool."

"And he did my movie, and he was nice to your little sister," I added.

"That's so true. I think I love him!" Sarah exclaimed, and then we laughed, and she said, "Speaking of which, I want to see the movie, except I might hate how I look and make you stop it, and I might have to talk about Curt. Wait a minute, does he look like a geek? Will this make me fall out of love with him? I like being in love. Or will this make me be more in love with him? I don't think I could stand to be even more in love, especially when I remember that he said no to going out for ice cream today."

"He's in the middle," I said, playing along. "You'll probably be equally in love with him after seeing this."

"And I might make you stop so I can say how great I think he is," Sarah interrupted me on my way to pressing the PLAY button. "Okay. Go ahead. Oh, the popcorn! Never mind, I'm still full of frog cake."

I pressed PLAY. Sarah couldn't stop talking, but I didn't mind. She was excited, and everything she said was a surprise, a good surprise. She noticed everything I was trying to do. She also couldn't get over how weird it was to see herself on film, though she didn't say it was a bad thing.

She also said that Curt looked really cute, and I thought she must be in love, since he had his mask on the whole time.

✿ CHAPTER TWENTY ✿

The Ecosystem of Romance

The next morning, we were awoken by a phone call for Dad. It was Joyce. Dad looked at me and Sarah as we walked into the kitchen and then said to Joyce, "Well, I *am* her legal guardian, otherwise known as her dad, so I can give you permission to do that. Yes, that would be nice." He was silent, and then he smiled. "Well, if it's a plan, it's a good thing Phyllis will help you with it!" After more listening, Dad said, "Okay, bye — hey — have I told you yet what a great mom you're going to be?" He looked at us and ran his fingers down his cheeks to show us that he'd made Joyce cry. We stifled our laughter. "Thank you, Joyce." He hung up.

"What was that about?" Sarah and I asked at the same time.

"Well, Miss You-Can't-See-My-Movie, I guess you'll have to wait and see!"

"That is so not fair," Sarah spoke up, which Dad enjoyed thoroughly.

"And why is that, Miss I-Got-To-See-The-Film?" he teased.

"Because that phone call was so obviously, totally about Amalee," she said.

"Well, I'm her father, so I get to decide what information to share with her. It's for her welfare, right?"

"No. You have to tell her, " Sarah insisted.

"I've got a secret, I've got a secret. . . ." Dad sang, and then disappeared.

Sarah suggested that we go flower picking. She said if we saw people in their lawns, we could ask them if they needed to have their flowers "thinned." "We can't steal them," she explained. "But flowers like tiger lilies multiply. We can even dig the plants out of the ground for people as a favor and keep the flowers. C'mon, it's good for us to talk to people."

She sounded like a combination of my dad, Phyllis, Joyce, and John. She didn't sound like Carolyn. Carolyn's idea of a good day would have no people. It would be to take two protein bars and get really lost in the woods and maybe end up sleeping under a tree.

"Alrighty," I agreed. "Let's get our trowels." I got the little shovels out of the garage and we set out. Kyle's truck was in the driveway. So was Kyle. He was wearing old shorts with paint stains all over them and a T-shirt with letters that were so faded I couldn't tell what they said. I could see his shoulder muscles through a hole in the sleeve. I sucked in my breath. After feeling jealous of Sarah around him, I now felt protected by her.

"Hey," she said, "where's your girlfriend?"

Or maybe I wasn't glad that she was here.

"Oh, uh, we broke up," he said.

"I'm sorry," Sarah said with enough sincerity for him, but not for me.

"It's fine. It was, uh, my idea."

"Not a very nice girl, was she?" Sarah asked.

"She wasn't *not* nice," I stammered, now horrified.

But Kyle laughed. How did Sarah get away with this stuff? "She was okay." He shrugged. I could tell he agreed with Sarah! Then he turned to me and asked, "Hey Amalee, how is the film going?"

"I finished it," I answered.

"It's awesome," Sarah told him.

"Let me know when I can see it!"

"You should," Sarah agreed. "Well, we're off on our travels!"

"Yeah, I've got to clip the hedges. Have a good one."

As we walked away, Sarah whispered, "Did you hear that? He's free! He's free! Hey, and don't be mad about what I said. I could have told him that she wasn't nice *or* smart."

"You are so bad!" I whispered back.

"I am your protectress," she corrected.

"Is that a word?" I asked.

"It should be."

I hoped that I wouldn't think about Kyle all the time the way Sarah thought about Curt. He was still much older. I realized that his news hadn't changed things much. If he ever asked me out on a date, I imagined all of Dad's friends would stand on the front step of our house, blocking me from coming out.

By the end of an hour, Sarah and I had tiger lilies, bachelor buttons, poppies, daisies, clover, and a bunch of other flowers we couldn't identify. We had also met people or found out where they lived, including, to my horror, Ms. Severence, who was just getting out of her car as we walked by. Sarah asked if we could thin her flowers.

"I don't have a lot of flowers," she pointed out.

"Yeah," I agreed. "We'll just leave you alone."

"No, wait a minute." She stopped us. "I'll give you some ferns. My ferns are out of control."

"We can thin them for you." Sarah held up her trowel. I almost groaned. I didn't want to crouch in Ms. Severence's lawn and drink the glass of water that she would offer, or use her bathroom, which Sarah would probably ask to do.

Ms. Severence laughed and said, "No, I don't need them uprooted. But those flowers are so pretty, I want to add something to the mix."

I loved how Ms. Severence had such a creative answer to our question. Instead of saying she had no flowers, she found a way to give us something else. She found a way to say yes.

That's the kind of thing she would have told us to do when we were her students: *Find a way to say yes*.

As we left, Sarah again leaned over and whispered, "So, is she going out with your dad?"

"No!" I hissed, giving her an exasperated look.

Sarah said, "Aren't you proud of me? I asked you instead of asking Ms. Severence."

I shook my head, but I couldn't deny how much I liked

Sarah's bravery. "You know what?" I told her. "If you hadn't told me to tape record my grandmother, I might not have made this movie. I think she was impressed that I brought the tape recorder."

"She *should have* been impressed by you. I wonder if she was freaked out, too. You told me you look like your mom, right?"

I liked how she called Sally my mom when she knew that we usually called her Sally. And she was right about my grandmother. She'd looked like she already knew me when she'd met me for the first time.

"She didn't get along with my mom," I said.

"That's too bad."

"It sounds like you get along with your mom, even though you don't see her all the time. You don't wish she and your dad were still together?"

"Hm, let me think about it," Sarah said sarcastically. "My dad is ten times happier with Lydia, and my mom is ten times happier with her new husband. My mom is nervous all the time, and Lydia is . . . Lydia. She goes on roller coasters with me. She tells me to speak up. She drives me everywhere. I don't even know if my mom still knows how to drive!"

"How does she get around, then?" I asked.

"She's *driven*," Sarah explained, and we chuckled. "Would you rather be with your mother than with your dad's friends? Seriously, would you?"

"No," I answered. "I don't know. I feel like if I missed my mom, my dad's friends would feel like they were bad parents." As soon as I said this, I knew it was why I couldn't ask them questions. Why would I want to ask about my mother if they were perfectly good parents?

"Maybe I'd want to have her out there somewhere, just to say hi every once in a while, but not instead of my dad's friends."

"That makes sense," said Sarah, looking distracted.

I had been letting Sarah lead us along on our flower walk . . . and suddenly I realized she'd taken us to Curt's house. I was amazed that I hadn't noticed all the flowers in front of it before. Was it our flower picking or the movie that made me notice now? "Hey!" I whispered. "Are we here just to look at Curt's house?"

"No, of course not!" Sarah protested. "No! Yes. Okay, I knew he lived here. But I wanted to pick flowers, and this seemed like a good way to go."

"I guess I'm lucky that Kyle is down the street. I know exactly what you're looking for."

"What am I looking for?"

"A car in the driveway," I began. "Stuff that he would

leave outside, like a baseball or a Frisbee. Somebody inside passing by a window. A look up the street and down the street to see if he's coming home." There *was* a car in the driveway. There was nothing that he'd left outside. We couldn't see in the windows. We looked up and and down the street. Curt was on his bike coming toward us! Even I felt excited.

"Hey," he said. "Twice in two days. Are you following me?"

Even though he was joking, Sarah was silent, for once, and I found myself jumping in.

"I just realized this was your house," I said. "You've got the greatest flowers! We were just out flower picking and it actually took me a minute to realize where we were."

"Me, too," Sarah said.

"You want some flowers?" Curt asked.

"No," I told him. "We're only taking leftovers from people's gardens. You know, things they've got too much of. And we should probably head home." I took some flowers from Sarah's arms to show that we already had so many. "We're going to John's restaurant. You want to come with us? My dad is going to take us there."

"No, that's okay," Curt said, backing up to get his bike into the driveway.

“See? What does he mean?” Sarah whispered.

“Why not?” I asked. Uh-oh. I kept going. “We finished the movie. You were great! And John is the chef, you know, the bullfrog. I’m sure he’d turn this into a big frog reunion.” Too bad we’d already had frog cake the night before.

Curt smiled. “Cool. But I’ve gotta go.”

As I told Sarah six or seven times on the way home, he didn’t sound mean or angry. I just thought he couldn’t get out of having dinner with his family.

“Or maybe he likes you and he was too surprised or freaked out to say yes on the spot like that,” I pointed out.

“No way. You think so, maybe?”

“I think so. Come to think of it, why would he be so nice to your little sister if he didn’t like you? Boys don’t do that.”

“Curt would.” Sarah sighed.

“This is like a science experiment,” I said. “We need more evidence. I’ll help you come up with more ways to run into him. I’ll show the movie to everyone who was involved.”

Sarah clasped her hands together and said, “Yesss!” Then she added, “What else are you going to do with your movie?”

A few days later, we had an answer. Joyce took me

down to the college to do last-minute editing and add the closing credits. She met Sandy and Karim. When I went out to the vending machines for chocolate bars, I came back to Joyce speaking quietly to them.

"You'll have to ask her," Karim was saying.

"Hey, Joyce, you're busted," Sandy added, pointing to me.

Joyce sighed. "Your dad said I could make a copy of the finished film, but they say it's up to you."

"Why do you want a copy?" I asked.

"I promise I wouldn't watch. I actually want a few copies to send to youth film festivals, or whatever they're called. I was going to surprise you. There are a few of them in the Northeast."

Karim said, "You should let Joyce do this for you. You're good at making movies. If you want to do more, this could, you know, it could . . ."

"Widen your horizons," Sandy finished.

"I was going to say, get you into a college with a good film program, but it's hard to say that to a thirteen-year-old," Karim explained.

"I'm twelve," I pointed out. Then I said yes to Joyce.

Before I could change my mind, Joyce turned to Karim and Sandy and said, "Ten copies. How fast?"

✿ CHAPTER TWENTY-ONE ✿

Myrtle on the Big Screen

And that is how my movie got chosen for the Young Hands-on Cameras Film Festival in New Haven, Connecticut, which apparently allowed my entry even though it was late. The screening itself was at the end of August, less than four weeks away.

I sent a mass e-mail to everyone. I sent an invitation on paper to Leslie Scott and her mom, who had been with me at the bank. I also, with Phyllis's blessing, put an invitation into Kyle's mailbox.

I went to the bank and gave an invitation to Ms. Hazlett, the teller. She said she could make it, and it turned out she wasn't the only one with space in her calendar.

Everyone was coming. Even John, who said he'd take

the night off. Even Marin's parents, as confused as they probably were by all of this.

Even Kyle. He came over to my house when I was out weeding with Dad and said, "I want to see your film. My mom wants me to go look at the Yale campus in New Haven. She says it will make me want to improve my grades."

"Do you want a ride?" Dad asked kindly.

"Uh, no, I'll drive," Kyle said with that new-license glimmer in his eyes. "But I'll see you there."

Dad called after him, "Tell your mom that SUNY New Paltz costs a third as much as Yale!"

And Kyle called back, "I don't think I'd get into either school, but thanks."

"Nice kid," Dad said. "Too old for you, of course."

"Yes," I said. "He *is* a nice kid."

"And too old for you," Dad repeated and laughed. He wouldn't let me get away with being mysterious on this one. Yes, toooo old.

When we finally arrived at the Young Hands-on Cameras Film Festival, on a humid night only a week before my first day of eighth grade, I wondered if I'd brought the whole audience. The festival was being held outside a park a little north of New Haven. The organizers put black curtains up all around the audience area so we could see the projection clearly. We would see four films total. Before the films started, I introduced myself to the people who ran the festival. I met the other kid filmmakers, who didn't seem like kids. They were a sixteen-year-old girl named Candace, another sixteen-year-old named Michael, and a fifteen-year-old boy named Amos, who was from Israel. We were very polite to each other. Amos's film was just before mine, which they'd chosen to go last.

I was going to sit between Sarah and Marin, but Marin was with her family in a shy, black-haired, quiet clump, and Sarah was sitting with Lydia, her sister Julie, and her dad on one side . . . and Curt on the other! When she caught my eye, I raised my eyebrows, but that's all. I didn't want Curt to see me. Sarah nodded her head to the side and I looked. There were Ms. Farraday and her husband, sitting with Hallie and her little sister, Anna. Leslie and her mom and dad were nearby. Then I saw what Sarah was looking at. There was my dad, and there was Ms. Severence sitting next to him, with her brother on her other side.

"Sit with us!" Joyce said, leading me over to Dr. Nurstrom and pushing me down between her and

Phyllis. Leslie and her mom came bounding over. Leslie asked why I hadn't asked for her help. I explained there weren't any real costumes. Then we talked about how classes were starting in a week, and who our teachers would be, and how cool this was and . . . Dad was sitting with Ms. Severence. We didn't talk about that.

I tried to concentrate on the films before mine. They all looked interesting, but I was thinking about how this huge crowd was about to see my film. I wanted my mom to be here . . . or did I want Sally? As a mom, it sounded like she would have shown up late and gotten all the attention by making people worry about her. Then I thought of Sally, the poetry-writing kid in her mother's car, the wide-eyed childlike person with the big butterflies on her shirt who seemed to think everything was beautiful. She came floating in from the woods with a crown of white flowers and a flowing pale dress with butterflies on it, saying, *Look everyone! Amalee made a movie about animals! I know you'll love it, because Amalee is a great girl, and you know what else? Believe it or not, they tell me she is my own daughter!* I couldn't really see her as a mother, but I wanted that feeling of being loved by her. It seemed like she could fill herself up with love for people. I realized I needed that right now. As Amos's film was ending, I wanted her to be with me.

Seeing the opening credits of my film helped to calm me. They looked so familiar after I'd spent an hour editing all the names onto the screen. There were the frogs, stretching out and taking their seats. The audience laughed. I saw it through their eyes. They were laughing with joy, and I laughed with them. When my name came up, my friends clapped. The audience was just like Sarah when she first saw it: Everything made them laugh and even point, but soon they got more serious. I hoped that Gail, Betsy, and Henry liked what I'd done with their interviews. Dave, the fish store guy, wasn't here. Too bad. He looked like a bad-boy movie star! I glanced over at Gail, who had shown up late with her husband-to-be. They had on the kind of shorts and shirts that people wear when they go camping, the kind that dry quickly and do all the things shirts need to do in a place like a reserve in India. They looked very happy together. Betsy was sitting with Carolyn and John, who seemed to be enjoying every minute of the film — except his own parts, when he would watch the film and wince. I guess he thought he looked fat. I'd have to tell him he was fabulous!

I looked over at Lenore when her part came up. She was punching her brother in the arm. He'd probably said something mean, which made me feel bad for Lenore. Her mom was nodding and smiling. She put her arm around Lenore. That was a good mom. I thought of Sally again. Maybe by now she would have settled down and been the best of Sally and a mother. Maybe she'd be sitting next to me on the grass, happy that she'd come back and seen me grow up and make my own movie. She'd put her arm around me and ask, "Isn't this amazing? I'm so glad I'm here with you."

Marin was back on the screen, looking like a tiny, matter-of-fact frog, explaining the importance of our fascination with nature. I was so thrilled when the butterflies raised their wings and the audience said, "Oooh!" And then, when Curt was talking about how the rosy periwinkle had raised the survival rate of infant leukemia by eighty percent, the audience made a surprised "OH!" Joyce turned and kissed her husband. Dr. Nurstrom nodded his head very seriously, then looked over at me and nodded again. It felt unexpectedly good to get the approval of a doctor. Doctors are scientists.

Finally, we got to Myrtle the sea turtle. Like Sarah, everyone leaned forward to hear her, just as I'd leaned closer to hear my grandmother. Myrtle said her philosophy.

Out of the corner of my eye, I saw Phyllis straighten her back. When Myrtle was done "talking," Phyllis and Joyce looked at each other over my head. Phyllis put her hand to her mouth. Joyce pulled out a tissue and dried a couple of tears. She had been crying throughout the movie, but this was different. Even I was amazed at how powerful this speech sounded. She seemed to have the entire audience convinced that they needed to look and listen more. I thought I might cry, too, just thinking about how many beautiful things we never even notice.

When Myrtle said "Good luck" at the end of the movie, there was a short silence, after which the applause exploded, followed by a standing ovation. I almost didn't need my mother, then. I was standing in a thunderstorm of love from the audience.

The film ended, and the festival president came out asking for a round of applause for all the filmmakers. The audience was still on its feet. All the filmmakers went up and took a bow, and the audience cheered. It was announced that I'd won second prize, and I was handed a check for two hundred and fifty dollars. Amos won first prize. Dad and Ms. Severence were both clapping, and when I saw Ms. Severence make a two-fingered whistle, I knew it was all over. Dad would fall in love with a woman who loved to read, loved to teach, and could do a two-fingered whistle. I just knew he would.

The tai chi people were cheering in a very unslow, un–tai chi–like way. Kevin even raised his fist. Maybe he had tiger energy.

And suddenly the neat little groups of people became a huge blur of mixed-up combinations as they came toward me. Marin and Betsy. Carolyn and Hallie next to Ms. Hazlett from the bank. A woman came up and told me she was from an environmental organization and wanted to use my film for their fund-raising dinner. It was too much.

Mr. Chapelle came over with John and put his hand on my shoulder. "William's asleep in the car with his mom, but I wanted to say what a wonderful movie that was. I'm honored that you used my film."

"I think I made my movie because of you!" I blurted.

Mr. Chapelle just nodded. John put his arm around him. "Oh, boy, crying in front of your students. AWK-ward!" This made Mr. Chapelle laugh, which I was relieved to see. It was so huge that he said this to me, but not so huge that I thought I could handle seeing him cry. I wanted to say something about how I wish he could work with less impossible people, like maybe tenth-graders, but hopefully my movie let him know that we had been listening to him, no matter what we'd pretended.

Dad came rushing over and picked me up. "Yahoo!" he whooped. "Amazing, sweetheart!"

John cried, "Put her down, David! You'll hurt your back!" Dad put me down. John swooped me up. "You've got to leave it to the experts. I've been working out!"

"You were fabulous, by the way," I told John. Mr. Chapelle agreed and slapped John on the back.

John looked at his stomach and said simply, "Why, thank you." I was proud of him for not asking if he looked okay.

Dad said, too casually, "Look who's here."

Kyle stepped out from behind Dad and John. I'd forgotten about Kyle! I'd been so distracted by Sarah and Curt and Phyllis and Henry and everyone. I'd looked for Kyle when I first got to the festival, but it had actually slipped my mind to look for him again. But then he smiled, and I was back to square one. There was no forgetting him in the long run. He was gorgeous.

"I can't believe you did that! You're the one who should go to Yale!" Kyle exclaimed, putting a hand on my shoulder. "How did you do all that research? You know so much stuff!"

I had the outrageous urge to ask him to drive me home just so I could keep listening to him. To him, I *was* the environmental scientist in the cool glasses showing him something in a microscope. I lost the urge when I realized I couldn't think of a thing to say past thanking him.

"Okay, a deal's a deal," Dad said to Kyle, then turned to me. "Kyle isn't supposed to be out after nine with his license. I told him I wouldn't bust him if he went right home."

"Yeah, I've got to go. Thanks, David. Congratulations, Amalee!" Kyle said, and then he put his arm around me before he disappeared. Not a real hug, but obviously something he wanted to do. I felt a sudden terror at the idea that he might ask me out on a date. Maybe I wasn't as in love with him as I thought. That was kind of a relief.

Dad said, "A very nice boy." Then he got serious as he changed the subject. "Amalee, honey, there's something else. . . ."

"Okay, ten thirty, into the car!" Phyllis ordered as she marched in from my left. "But before we go . . ." She nodded to Dad and they whisked me off to the side.

"You see, Amalee . . ." Dad began.

"Was that who I thought it was?" Phyllis asked quietly. I remembered the look that Phyllis and Joyce had exchanged. I knew what she was asking.

"I couldn't get a permission slip to use her voice," I said. "She had already died."

Phyllis made an exasperated laugh. "That's not why I'm asking. So that *was* your grandmother?"

"Yes. I taped her."

"She let you?" Dad asked. "Wow." He shook his head.

Phyllis looked at both of us. "You need to know something, Amalee. What do you think she was talking about when she talked about losing things before they could teach her anything, or about how she regretted that she'd let go of some things forever?"

"I don't know," I said. "The world. It seemed like the kind of thing you say to someone when you're old and about to die."

Phyllis paused. "What do you think she might have been referring to? What had she overlooked?"

I thought about it a second. And I knew. . . .

"Sally," I whispered. Of course she was talking about Sally. Of course. I thought about where I'd put my grandmother's speech in the movie. It was when we were talking about Frog X. That was it. Sally, the child who wouldn't grow up, the non-mom who I didn't want to talk about because she'd been replaced already, the alcoholic, the one we never talked about, the one who left before I could ever know her. The one who deserved better than to be forgotten, extinct from our memories. Sally was Frog X, and I'd known it the whole time.

Phyllis started to cry. Dad put his hand over his eyes and looked miserable. "Poor Sally," Phyllis whispered. "What would she have given to hear her mother say that?"

Dad cleared his throat and pretended that he hadn't been crying himself. "It's so late," he said. "We've got to get home."

Joyce wandered over. Just past her, I saw the world was still going, filled with the surprises of living people. Karim and Sandy were holding hands. Ms. Severence was clearly waiting for Dad. Gail and her fiancé were zipping up their matching coats.

"We're setting out," Joyce began, then saw us looking very quiet and serious. "Oh, goodness. So it *was* her, the tortoise?"

"Turtle. Tortoises only live on the land," I quietly corrected her. Joyce reached for her tissue. I was already walking away.

I found a particularly tall and stately tree just out of the light, and I started to cry. Soon they were calling my name, and I knew I had to go. I got myself under control and headed over to them. I, too, had lost Sally before she could teach me something, whether she was the happy, floating child-fairy or the mom who was excited for me to do the things she'd always wanted to do. I wondered who this person was, and whether she held some secrets I might have needed. I'd spent so long telling myself that Sally was a fun girl but not important to me.

But she *was* important, if unknown. Just like Frog X.

✿ CHAPTER TWENTY-TWO ✿

A Frog Remembered

The phone started ringing around eight in the morning.

Carolyn didn't even bother to identify herself. "Betsy wants to take you to Ecuador on her next trip. If you want to go, don't drink the water or even eat the fruit. I just thought I'd warn you."

"Ecuador?" I asked. "Do you think I could go?"

"Not in a million years. Your dad wouldn't let you. Also, I think there was just a big takeover in the government. But if you do get to go, I'll take you to get your shots so you don't get all those rain forest diseases. Hey, your movie was even better on that big screen." She hung up and I thought about whether *I* would let me go to Ecuador, let alone Dad.

Of all people, Hallie called a little later.

"Am I calling too early?" she asked.

She said she thought the film was beautiful and that her little sister had stayed awake for the first half hour of the trip home saying that she was a movie star, but she wished she could be a panther when she grew up. We both laughed, and I said, suddenly, "I'm sorry Ellen moved away. That must have been hard for you."

And she answered, just as suddenly, "Amalee, when we stole your books as an April Fool's joke, I felt so bad. It was really terrible that we did it. And . . . was that the reason you pushed Lenore down the stairs, because you were upset?"

I remembered that terrible day when Ellen and Hallie had stolen the notebooks I needed for the only two classes I cared about, both with Ms. Severence.

"I was upset," I admitted slowly. "But I was more upset at Lenore, because she told me my father was dying."

"I know," she said quickly. "I know the whole story. Ellen did, too, but I was thinking that we just made your life so hard that day, on top of the whole Lenore thing, and I don't know why. When you pushed Lenore right after we'd stolen your books, I felt like it was my fault."

"It wasn't," I said, astounded. "It wasn't." I didn't know what else to say, but I decided to say something that showed I considered her to be a friend. "So, did you see my dad sitting with Ms. Severence?" I asked.

"Yeah!" she cried. "Was that weird for you? I mean, I liked her a lot. I guess if he's going to like a teacher, she's a good choice. But — *agh* — so weird!" Then she added, "Did you see Curt and Sarah? I noticed you weren't sitting with them. Was this like a date for them?"

My call-waiting beeped and I looked to see who it was. "I should probably go," I told Hallie. "That's Sarah, so I guess I'll find out about Curt. If she and I go swimming today, you want to come?"

"I'd love to," Hallie said.

I clicked to Sarah. "Tell me," I demanded.

Sarah laughed. "Well, I'll tell you this. He came over and sat with me."

"I am *so* not surprised!" I said.

"And his leg touched mine, and he didn't pull it away. He laughed with everyone else when I first got up and put my hands on my hips. And that's it. But he's in two of my classes this year, so I won't have to hunt him down anymore."

"What happened when the two of you left?" I asked.

"Nothing, but he was with his dad, and I was with Dad and Lydia, so there was no way. But get this — I think he wanted something to happen."

"How do you know?"

"He just looked at me like that."

"Wow, he did?" This was so exciting. This was more exciting than Ecuador. I thought about Sarah's stepmom thinking I only cared about plants and turtles. If only she knew!

"So now I feel pretty relaxed. I'll just see what happens at school."

School started on Tuesday. Today was Saturday. Couldn't I skip school and just go to college? Why did I have to stop to learn algebra? I told Sarah I was very happy for her, and, since I was getting another call-waiting beep, I signed off.

It was Phyllis. "How are you doing today?" she asked without saying hello.

"I'm fine. I might go to Ecuador. And Hallie apologized for stealing my books last year. And Sarah's in a good mood."

Phyllis chuckled and said, "I saw those cute little froggies sitting together last night." Then she continued, "Are you too overwhelmed for a short road trip with me and Joyce tomorrow?"

"No," I answered — and was interrupted by another beep. Who could this be? I looked at the call waiting. A number I didn't recognize. I got off and talked with Kevin, the tai chi guy, who said thanks and invited me to do tai chi with them if I wanted. I thought I couldn't move that slowly unless I was watching television, but I said I'd consider it.

When I hung up, the phone rang again. It was Dad. "Hey, I thought you were here!" I told him.

"I'm getting some things at the farmer's market with John. He had to go really early, and I didn't want to wake you. How are you? Has Phyllis called yet? Are you up for a trip tomorrow?"

I said I was. He said he'd be home soon and make celebration omelets with those enchanted mushrooms John had used before.

I decided to work off some of my energy by taking a bike ride to the library to return some of my research books. As I started to pedal, I realized I shouldn't have been so afraid of my wild blood. It was fun to go so fast. It was fun to feel alive. Sally had loved being alive. I knew she had. She would have loved the weather today. She would have laughed at the big dog that was tearing through the long grass. She would have admired the giant oak tree at the side of the road. I did all these things for her.

I came home and listened to nine messages: Betsy; Mrs. Nielson, thanking me on behalf of Lenore; Joyce; Joyce again; Marin, who said she loved the movie and so did her parents; Henry from the aquarium; Sarah again; Phyllis again; and Ms. Severence, who called herself *Ann*

Severence and said, "I'm sorry I didn't get a chance to congratulate you last night. I just ran into your dad at the farmer's market." Oh, yeah, like Sarah just ran into Curt at the swimming hole! Was Ms. Severence tracking down my dad? Was he tracking *her* down? ". . . And he said you were home, but I guess you've stepped out. I just wanted to say you did a great job. And I'm not surprised. You've got a big heart and a great mind. Okay, that's all. Bye, Amalee."

I sighed. She still made me nervous, just because I liked her. If she and Dad were together somehow, even if they became friends, could I get over this? I'd have to, I guessed.

Dad came home with two canvas bags filled with vegetables and a big bouquet of black-eyed Susans. I put the flowers in water while he cleaned the mushrooms.

"We'll have to decide what you want to do now," he said. "Do you want to be a filmmaker, a scientist, an environmental activist, or a writer?"

"Yes," I said.

Dad laughed and explained, "I didn't know I had such a firecracker on my hands. I feel like I'm supposed to start signing you up for things like special camps or after-school programs, right?"

"Don't you think you've done enough?" I asked. "Think about what I learned this summer."

"You're a brave girl," Dad muttered. "You got that from Sally." Hadn't Phyllis said that? "But I want to help you focus your talents," he continued.

"So I don't end up like Sally?" I asked.

Dad stopped cracking eggs and looked at me. Whoops. He looked up at the ceiling and answered, "Yes, that's exactly why I want to help you, to tell the truth, but not in the way you think. Sally was smart, and her parents didn't do anything to help her focus her mind. She wouldn't believe me when I told her how bright she was. So I want to be in the right place at the right time to help you. Do you have an idea of what you want to do next?"

"How about Ecuador? Next dugout boat leaves in a week."

Dad surprised me by saying, "If, in a couple years, you wanted to go to Ecuador with Betsy Wright and Carolyn, we could discuss it."

"I'm not sure I could handle all the shots. I'd settle for learning more about filmmaking."

"You got it." Dad exhaled with relief. "I was lying. I'd never let you go to Ecuador with Carolyn! Ann's other brother — Ms. Severence's other brother — just came up from the city. He might know about film programs in New York next year. You're still a bit young, probably."

"So I hear you saw Ann at the farmer's market."

"How did you know that?" Dad asked, alarmed.

"She called."

"What did she call about?" Dad started walking to the phone.

"I erased it. It was for me. She said congratulations."

"Oh," Dad murmured, coming back to the kitchen. "John told me he always sees her at the farmer's market." So Dad *was* tracking her down! My experience with Kyle had taught me all I needed to know. This was real.

"So I guess the two-fingered whistle sealed the deal, huh?" I asked. "Ms. Severence knows how to whistle like a football fan."

Dad smiled admiringly and said, "I could never do that. What do you mean 'sealed the deal'?"

"That's what made you want to sneak out early and go to the farmer's market. Just like that first moment when you knew how you felt about Sally, when she put her arms around you and Phyllis and said she wanted to be friends. And kissed you on the cheek."

Dad looked me in the eye. "Good memory," he said. "I like Ms. Severence. I know that you found her first."

At that we both laughed, which loosened things up

enough for Dad to say, "If she starts coming around here more, I will do everything I can to make it not weird. Would that be all right?"

"You'll be too busy looking at her," I told him.

"No, I won't."

"It *is* weird," I admitted. "I'm sorry."

"I'd tell you I wouldn't see her, but I don't think you'd want that. You wouldn't want me to live with a big lie like that. I know you. You're the kind of person who visits the grandmother who disowned Sally and tape-records her!"

"That was Sarah's idea," I told him. I'd meant to tell him last night that I was sorry I did it behind his back.

"So what do you think?" Dad asked.

"Invite her to John's on Monday night," I said.

"Oh, no, that's okay. That's the last night before school."

"I'll invite Sarah to make sure there's no lack of conversation," I said. "And you invite Ann. You're right. Let's do this. We'll get it out in the open. Should I call her?"

"Wow, do you want to?" Dad asked.

"I want to call her like you wanted me to go to Ecuador," I said.

"Ah, I see. I'll call."

We drove to New Paltz that afternoon and got some

new school supplies. We talked about what people need to do to help endangered species. Dad felt like a friend, or a fellow teacher — a "colleague," as he said of the people he worked with.

In the late afternoon we got home and I watched a movie that Henry had given Dad for me. It was all about sea turtles. I was interested, but I started getting sleepy.

Dad laughed as I dragged through dinner. "You're crashing from last night's excitement," he explained.

After dinner I started reading a book I'd gotten out of the library, but soon I was fast asleep.

I awoke to three faces looking over me. Phyllis's face said, "Dr. Nurstrom's waiting in the car."

"I wish you'd call him Robert!" Joyce's face exclaimed. Then she noticed, "Wow, you really crashed, didn't you?"

"I made you breakfast, sweetheart," Dad's face said.

Soon we were all heading out to the car, with me pulling on a sweatshirt while Phyllis held my toast. "Notice," she said, "that we put cashew butter on this instead of peanut butter. Cashews are grown and harvested in the rain forest, so buying cashew butter supports people in the rain forest who might otherwise let their trees be cut down for farmland. We're trying to do our part."

"Not before my coffee, please," I complained.

"How about hot chocolate?" Dad asked, putting a travel mug in my hand. I noticed he had also grabbed the black-eyed Susans. Where were we going?

"Carolyn said she's sorry she couldn't come, but, well, we'll discuss it later," Joyce said.

For the next fifteen minutes we listened to news on public radio. We crossed the Hudson River.

Phyllis cleared her throat. "You know . . ." she started. "How are you doing? Still hungry? Want to go back to sleep?"

"I'm fine."

Phyllis continued. "I never actually disliked your mother. Your dad says he told you the rock-climbing story. I was annoyed. But I didn't dislike her. And she did have a problem, so I was worried about both her and your dad when they got married."

"It was hard to dislike her," Joyce continued. "She had a spark. She really seemed to love the world the way a child would. I envied that."

"She did," Phyllis agreed.

Dad turned to me and said, "She told me once that she wanted to do something really great for the world. She just didn't know what it would be."

"Gosh, why couldn't she stick around long enough

to find out she did give something great to the world?" Phyllis snorted, talking to Dad. "I mean, isn't that the biggest coincidence? She leaves us all behind, because she's afraid she'll miss out on this great thing she wants to do. But she left the great thing with us. She gave us Amalee."

I thought of how much work it had taken for Dad's friends to convince me I was worth anything when I was in the sixth grade. I could imagine thinking, like Sally did, that I'd had to go to an entirely new place to do anything right. I would have to start all over. "Maybe she didn't like herself, and she thought she had to leave so she could change into something she liked," I suggested.

Dad nodded. "That is exactly what it was, Ama. And she gave us more than you. She gave us herself. She was a really fun, loving girl. And she was an alcoholic. It's amazing how many friends I've had who have stopped drinking. I wonder what it would be like today if Sally had stopped and were still here."

I thought of Frog X.

"Anyway, Ama, we saw your movie, put our heads together, and decided we should let you know more about her," Dad said. He handed me the black-eyed Susans. "First of all, these were her favorite flowers."

I felt my eyes tearing up already. Was it because I remembered the supermarket receipt with the flowers?

I could see a kid with long hair, shorts and boys' white socks running down the aisle to add this to her mother's groceries at the check-out line. "Pleeease?" she was asking.

Or maybe it was that the black-eyed Susan was such a simple flower. I thought of how she called her mother's awards and degrees "fancy prizes." She stuck up for unfancy things and said they were the most beautiful. They were also cheap and easy to find. They were the kind of thing your husband could get for you even if he wasn't rich. She didn't need a boat or a big house or a giant bottle of champagne. She *was* Frog X. But she was also the kind of person who cared about Frog X, the unflashy, the unwealthy. Didn't Dad say she loved animals?

We crossed the line into Connecticut. We took the same exit we had taken for my grandmother's house.

Joyce turned to me and said, "Honey, we're going to take you someplace. We'll be with you the whole time. We're with you."

"I think this is the right thing to do," Dad said.

Ahead were the gates to a big cemetery.

"She's buried here," I said. I didn't even have to ask. "I'm bringing flowers to leave at her gravestone."

"Yes," Dad said. "If you want. We're all going. You can stay in the car, but I thought you'd want to go."

I didn't want to look at the gravestone with Dad's friends. I didn't even want to go with my dad. They didn't know the same girl I knew, the one with the flowers and the barrettes and the rhymes and even the way she loved the big champagne bottle full of coins. "Can I go alone?" I asked.

"I thought you might ask to do that." Dad sighed.

"And?"

"Just a minute." Dad and Phyllis ran out and found a directory at the entrance of the cemetery that they scanned. I could tell they were discussing my request.

Joyce said, "Do you really want to do this alone?"

"Absolutely," I said.

"Why?" Joyce asked.

"It's my mother."

Phyllis and Dad got back in the car.

"She's going alone," Joyce told them.

"You think that's a good idea?" Phyllis asked.

"I don't know, but it's her idea, and it's her right. It's her mother," Joyce said, echoing me.

Dad and Phyllis took this under consideration and then nodded in agreement.

Dad said, "I am more than happy to go with you, just me, and I actually would prefer it."

"And it would be safer," Phyllis added.

"I'll do it alone," I said.

"Okay. We'll drive up the road. We'll never have you out of our peripheral vision if you want to flag us down," Phyllis said.

"Here we are," Dr. Nurstrom said nervously.

"Is this too much?" Dad asked.

I didn't know if it was too much. "No," I said.

"I'm the therapist. Blame it on me. I say she can handle it," Joyce said, coming out to open my door for me.

Dad walked over to a small, plain gravestone and looked at it. He shook his head. "There it is," he said. I stood next to him and saw the name. Within the cluster of shiny stones that said WESTON was SALLY WESTON. There was her whole name and the dates she was alive, 1970–1994.

It was the best evidence I'd ever had that she'd been alive, better than the receipts or even the flowers I was holding. She didn't just live in stories.

"I'm going to the car," Dad said. "We'll leave you for fifteen minutes. I know myself. I can't bear to leave you any longer than that."

Dad knew me, too. He knew I liked to take things on alone at first. Dad walked to the car, and Dr. Nurstrom slowly drove away.

I couldn't be silent as I looked at Sally's name, so I

took a breath and reminded myself that nobody was going to tell me I sounded stupid. “Hi, Sally,” I started. “These are for you. They’re from my — from David.” I put the flowers down. The simple gravestone matched the simple wildflowers. “I am Amalee. I am your daughter, and as you know, we never knew each other. I hardly even knew about you until this summer. I’m actually sorry about that. I wish I’d asked more about you. And I met your mother, too. And you know what? She was sorry, too. She wanted to know you better. When she died, she left me . . . guess what she left me? She left me that bottle of coins. And she told me to spend it now.” I told her I’d just made a movie about endangered species with the money from the huge bottle of coins. I could barely see the car up ahead, and I felt very alone with this unshiny, simple gray gravestone. “I’m not angry that you left and all that,” I blurted out, afraid that I didn’t have much longer to talk. This was the closest I’d ever come to speaking to her. “I know about your problem. But you didn’t do anything bad to me. I don’t need a mother, because all the people you knew who went to college with Dad are still around: John, Carolyn, Joyce, and Phyllis. They’re always at the house. Or we go to John’s restaurant, which is awesome. They say they really like doing parent things with me. It really works the way it is. But, of course, I am your daughter."

That did it. That's when I sat down and started to cry. I traced her name with my finger. I was her daughter. There would be plenty of time for me to go back to talking about that girl named Sally I'd never known, but I let things be different today. And as crazy as it was, I knew one thing was true. The secret was out. I loved my mom.

I heard footsteps behind me and wheeled around in terror. It was Dad. I didn't have time to dry my tears.

"You scared me!" I said.

"Sorry," he panted. He caught his breath and hugged me. It almost felt like a big John hug. "She really was special," he said, resting his cheek on the top of my head for a moment. "She just didn't feel . . . finished. I have a hard time remembering her as a person, because I spent so much time hoping that she would become the person she wanted to be."

"She was a person," I said.

"Yeah, she was. And I was so caught up in trying to help her, I didn't help her. I saw her as a problem to solve, like a fixer-upper."

"I understand why you would try to help," I told him.

"Sure. But I regret that I never treated her like a

person to you. You have a right to know you had a mother, not a silly Sally who never grew up. She was your mother. And you also have the right to imagine what it would have been like if she had stayed and been your mom."

"I have thought of that, sometimes," I admitted.

"Do you need more time?" Dad asked.

I looked over at the flowers and at her name. A door had closed. I couldn't imagine talking to the gravestone and believing that anyone could hear me. I'd said what I needed to say, and now she was a young woman named Sally again. "We can go," I said, but my visit had been a very good idea. I knew that I would never feel completely separate from her again.

At lunch, Joyce talked about decorating the baby's room, clearly getting away from the topic of my mother and cemeteries. "Guess what I'm thinking of for the wallpaper?" she asked me. "Frogs. Little smiling bullfrogs. It's just a coincidence, but I think that's perfect. When little person is old enough, I'll tell him or her about Amalee's important movie."

"I'll teach him or her how to use a camera. Once I've learned, of course," I said.

"Ama's going to take some film classes," Dad said.

"I'll film little person, too," I told Joyce and Dr. Nurstrom.

"Thank you," said Dr. Nurstrom. He, too, used the expression *little person* that Joyce had come up with. "We'd love to have some footage of little person, and I'm no good with cameras."

"How would you like to make a film about childbirth?" Joyce asked.

"I think I'll stick to environmental science for now," I said. "Maybe I'll change my mind."

I thought about Joyce on the way home. She was not like my mother. She was so excited about having a baby that she'd picked out special towels, pillows, and rugs. That didn't make me feel sorry for myself, though, because Joyce had been just as excited about me. I still remembered when she took me shoe shopping. I was four. She asked if I wanted a matching purse.

Sarah was waiting for me on the front step as we pulled in the driveway.

We all apologized as we got out of the car. I had totally forgotten that she was coming.

Sarah waved us all off and said she'd already let herself in and gone through our refrigerator. Joyce said that sounded like a good idea and headed inside. Sarah tugged my arm and walked me away from the house in the other direction from Kyle's house, possibly because his truck was in his driveway.

"Guess who I talked with?" Sarah asked, speeding me towards the same hill I'd wiped out on.

"Curt?"

"Just now," Sarah said.

"Kyle?"

"Uh-huh. Guess who we talked about? You." Sarah answered herself.

I held still. This was another time I wanted to hear the whole story without distractions.

Sarah said it went something like this:

Sarah asked, "So, Amalee's movie was pretty great, wasn't it?"

"She's a genius," Kyle said.

"And didn't she look so great when she was standing up there at the end, getting her award?"

"She's pretty," Kyle answered. "And in a couple years, she's going to be a knockout."

I wanted to jump up and down, but I saw Sarah was already doing it for me. "Pretty! Pretty! I mean, I think you're pretty, too, but he said it."

"But I'm not a knockout," I pointed out, still happy that he even thought about the way I looked.

"Oh, please, you know that we're going to look better in high school. And by the way, isn't it cool that he thinks you're a genius?"

We stepped to the side of the road to let a car pass, but it slowed down instead. We turned to see Kyle opening the passenger window. "You guys need a ride?" he asked.

Sarah and I started laughing. No, it was giggling. We were definitely twelve years old. "No, thank you," I said as seriously as I could. I got a sudden pang of fear thinking what would happen if Kyle actually asked me on a date. I suddenly decided I would wait for a while before that happened. I could see how I was feeling after I got my braces off. I'd probably wear them for a year. I felt better. Wait a year.

Kyle drove off with a friendly smile, completely unaware of the decision I'd made. No Kyle. At least, not yet.

When we got home, Sarah laid out the three outfits she was thinking of wearing to school the next day. We decided that she would wear blue pants with a green shirt and I would wear green pants with a blue shirt, so that if we were having a bad first day, we could remember that we weren't alone, but not matching so much that we stood out. I thought of Ellen in my head saying that our idea was ridiculous, but then I thought of Hallie wishing she could wear matching clothes like a secret code on the first day, too. Things had really changed.

We went to dinner at John's restaurant. Dad had invited Ms. Severence, as I'd given him permission to do. She was at the restaurant, along with Carolyn, Phyllis, Joyce, Dr. Nurstrom, and, of course, John, who was starting a new menu to welcome the fall.

Phyllis asked us what we were hoping would happen in the eighth grade, and we lied. Sarah wanted Curt to say he was head-over-heels in love with her, and I was hoping my science teacher would move or go to jail or something. Everyone knew she was crazy, but it wasn't the kind of thing I would say to adults. Sarah and I said we hoped we liked algebra.

"You're going to love it," Phyllis said passionately.

Ms. Severence said, "It's such a fine line. On the one hand, it's important for me to know what I want the school year to be, but then again, I always have to remind myself not to let my expectations get in the way of enjoying what actually happens." What an un-Sally thing to say. I looked over to see what Dad thought of this. He was nodding and frowning. I think he was frowning for me, just to prove that he wouldn't be showing any signs of being in love tonight. I also noticed that he and Ms.

Severence never touched each other once. They didn't even sit next to each other. Ms. Severence looked over and smiled at me. I could almost see her as not a teacher. That was a start.

The next morning, Sarah and I headed for school on foot. There was a path through the woods behind my house, the same woods where I'd heard the peeping frogs and thought they should narrate a movie. This summer was a story that was better than my expectations. We emerged from the woods to see a traffic jam of busses and cars and hundreds of kids pouring out of them.

"Hello, eighth grade," Sarah muttered.

"Wow. It's so busy," I said.

"Yeah," Sarah agreed. Then she laughed. "You know what they look like to me? They look like frogs. Look at those two little tree frogs who are very fascinating, indeed." She pointed to a pair of twins, all in pink, emerging from the back of a car. They held hands for a second, then dropped them, realizing that they didn't want to be called babies on their first day at this new school. Beautiful frogs.

"Oh, and look, there's the actual Frog X!"

"Where?" I asked, wishing I could see Sally in her white socks and sparkly hair clips, but Sarah was just pointing to Lenore, who had stepped off the bus looking ready for the worst. Or was she? She didn't have her books clamped as tightly to her chest as she had last year.

Sarah was right about how it all looked. I could see the whole school as frogs: climbing, jumping, peering out of windows, and bouncing on the sidewalks, the skinny leopard frogs, the big bullfrogs, the glittering poison dart frogs, and the awkward frogs that didn't have any particular markings or colors.

"There's a mutated frog." Sarah pointed to a boy on crutches.

"Sarah!" I said.

"It's not a bad thing. I'm the two-headed frog. He's my brother!" Sarah protested.

I sighed. "Ready for this?" I asked, heading toward my homeroom.

"Sure!" Sarah joked. Then she took my hand and squeezed it before she headed in the other direction.

So much had changed in two years. I had friends. I had things that I wanted to do. I had plans to take a film course. My favorite sixth-grade teacher wanted to be my new friend. And all of these kids, instead of looking like a big mass of trouble I'd have to wade through to reach the other end of eighth grade, were interesting to me. Who would they be this year? Some of them held the answers to important questions. One of them might invent a cure for cancer because of something he learned in science class. One of them might need us to notice her. It was impossible to know who would be important to me, and why, and who I might be important to.

For all the things I couldn't predict, however, I had the gift of knowing that, as I headed into this crowded school, this massive rain forest, this endangered world, the everythingness of everything, all I could do, and all I had to do, was listen and watch and learn.